THE DEVIL WEARS TIMBS 2

THE REALEST KILLAZ
A NOVEL BY TRANAY ADAMS

The Devil Wears Timbs 4

The Devil Wears Timbs 4/ Tranay Adams-1st ed. © 2016

Kindle Formatting: MADE Write

Editor: The Ghost

Cover Artist: Sunny Giovanni

Publisher: Tranay Adams

THE DEVIL WEARS TIMBS IV

Prologue

Annabella Bemmy sat behind her desk staring at a portrait of her and her father. Tears slowly rolled down her cheeks as fond memories of them went through her mind. Her lips curled down at their ends and she sniffled, snatching a couple of Kleenex tissues from the box on her desktop. After dabbing her eyes dry she blew her nose and wiped it. She then sat the portrait down on the desktop and balled up the soiled tissue, throwing it into the waste basket that was sitting not too far away. Annabella had never been the toughest girl, but when she lost her father four years ago it changed her drastically. In her heart she knew that she had to become just as calculated, cunning and ruthless as him if she was going to take over his business, and that's exactly what she did. She could have let the business perish along with her father but she believed that he would want her to carry on the torch. She felt this way because she overheard him talking about grooming one of the young men from his organization to become his heir. It was because of this that she decided to put her dreams on hold in order to honor her old man's name and his proceedings.

"Ms. Bemmy, there is a Julian King waiting out in the lobby to see you." a voice rang out from the intercom loud and clear.

"Okay, give me a second." she spoke as she held the button down. She then pulled open the top desk drawer, removing a pocket size mirror and a makeup kit. Once she'd straighten up her makeup, which her crying had ruined, she stored the items away and closed the drawer.

Annabella held down the button to the intercom and spoke. "Send him in."

2

Quickly, she put on her signature scowl when it was time to handle business and steepled her hands in her lap, resting them on top of her long, sexy legs. Anytime she was around anyone in the lifestyle she always made sure to carry herself a certain way. She did this because a lot of the men in the business looked at women as inferior to them. There was no way in hell she was going to have them look at her anyway other than they did each other. Her aura had to give off wealth, power, sophistication and prestige whenever she was in their presence. It was from her attitude and actions that her colleagues christened her *The Pitbull In A Skirt.*

A moment later the double doors of the office opened and in walked Julian King. He was a tall, slender man with a slight muscular build. He was easy on the eyes, clean shaven and wore his long brunette hair pulled back in a ponytail. Today he was dressed in a brown leather coat which he wore over a button-down shirt and a tie. A pair of wire rimmed glasses framed his eyes. He wore a simple Timex watch on his wrist and a wedding band on his finger. From the way that he was dressed it would be easy for someone to mistake him for one of those yuppies that worked on Wall Street, but that couldn't be further from the truth. This mothafucka here was a straight up coldblooded killer by trade. He was trained to go. There wasn't anyone on the face of the planet that he wouldn't bring it to for the right price.

"Mr. King, please have a seat." Annabella outstretched her hand toward the chair sitting beyond her desk. "I hope you have some good news for me." she placed her elbows on the desktop and put her fingers and thumbs together, leaning forward to give him her undivided attention.

3

"I'm afraid not," he admitted, removing his glasses and pulling a cloth from inside of his coat. He went onto fog up the lenses with his hot breath and cleansed them while he talked. "I've searched everywhere for Mr. Simpson. I can't seem to find anything on him, which I'm not surprised given the regards to who has trained him."

Annabella shut her eyelids and bowed her head, taking a very deep breath hating to have heard the disappointing news. Taking the time to calm down, she looked back up into the eyes of the killer. In them she saw nothing, they were soulless and his narrow face was expressionless. She couldn't read him at all. All she knew was that he was good at what he did which was the reason why she'd paid the half of million dollars he'd requested for his services. The amount of money he wanted was obscene, but with his credentials and background she felt that he was worth every dollar, especially since he'd guaranteed her that he could execute Fearless.

"Mr. King, I sure do hate to hear you say that." Annabella took the time to pour up a glass of Cognac. Once she was done she plugged the bottle and set it aside, swirling the dark liquor around inside of her glass as she stared ahead at her visitor. "I've paid you a hell of a lot of money 'cause I was assured that you could bring me Mr. Simpson dead or alive. It's been what? Two weeks now? And you still haven't found him? I'm sorry to say that I'm starting to believe that you were blowing smoke up my ass when you told me that you were the best there was at what you do." Hearing this caused Julian to scowl and square his jaws, making them pulsate they were so tight. If it was one thing he hated it was his level of expertise being questioned. In his profession he had killed many, many men and he'd never been given a contract that he couldn't fulfill. It was

4

always one shot one kill, and he always got his man for that matter.

"You'll get ya man, I just needa lil' more time," he assured her, "In fact, I have someone that is going to point me in the right direction of our lil' friend."

"Is that right?" she laid back in her executive chair, crossing her legs and placing her fingertips together.

"Positive." he nodded. "If you don't mind me asking, why is it that chu want this guy's head so bad?"

"If you may know, Mr. King, he killed my father."

Annabella's father was the late kingpin, Niles Bemmy. He was the head of a drug operation called The West Coast Connection. This organization of some of the most powerful men in Southern California had Fear on their payroll as a hit-man. The relationship between the killer and the The Connection was fine. That was until their supplier learned of his murdering of a very close friend of his and ordered them to sever all ties to him. Feeling disrespected, Fear vowed to dismantle the five men collective and that he did, finishing off Annabella's father last. After her father had been murdered at his restaurant, she ran the tapes back and zoomed in on his killer's face. That's when she discovered that Al Simpson aka Fearless was responsible and hired the same assassin that her father had in mind, United Kingdom's own, Julian King.

After her father's murder, Annabella dropped out of school and took over the family business. She now sat at the table with the successors of the West Coast Connection with her being the head of the entire empire. They still had the same supplier and business was running as smooth as ever. Once she had solidified her father's business, she searched through her old man's rolodex for the killer that he and his associates had spoken so highly of. It was then that she placed a phone call to require his services. Julian King knew exactly who Annabella Bemmy was; he was just surprised that he'd gotten that phone call so many years later. Nonetheless, he took her upon her offer and so far he had been out in Killa Cali for two weeks. She insisted that he relaxed before he went about the task of finding her father's murderer, but he wouldn't hear of it. He got straight down to business trying smoke out the son of a bitch that had been responsible for whacking out the most powerful ensemble out there on The Left Coast.

"I assure you I feel your pain." he twisted the wedding band on his finger back and forth. "I lost my wife and kid years ago."

For many years Julian King pretended to be a college professor when he was really a freelance hit man. His family had no idea what he actually did for a living but one day his secret came to light. Julian came home after a job to find his family sitting on the couch. Their mouths were gagged and their wrists and ankles were duct taped. Three men surrounded them. Their leader stood at the back of them, gun in his hand ready to give their innocent asses some funerals.

Flashback

"Sit da briefcase down," Jayo ordered, pointing his gun to the back of Monica's head. This was the hit-man's wife. Her eyes were running with wetness and she looked terrified.

"What's going on here?" Julian's forehead indented with a crease. His head snapped from left to right, taking in the hard faces of the larcenous men standing inside of his living room.

Jayo's hand shot up into the air and he let one off into the ceiling, debris fell. The single shot startled Julian's

6

wife and their eight year old son J.J. He was crying and snot nosed, green bubbles forming out of his nostrils.

"Put da goddamn briefcase down, or da next won is goin' into da back of ya wife's pretty liddle head." he gritted, pressing that steel to the back of old girl's thinking cap.

Julian threw up a surrendering hand and slowly bent his knees to sit his briefcase down. "Okay, alright, I'm doing it now."

"Good, boy." he glared at him through the strands of his long, greasy black hair as he did as he was told. A creepy smile parted his thin, pink lips. "You do know why we're here, right?"

"Nah, no, I'ma teacher. I don't have anything to do with the criminal element."

"Criminal element?" the cat standing to Jayo's right lifted an eyebrow. He exchanged glances with his comrades and they all busted up laughing at Julian's bullshit.

"Boy, I'll tell ya," Jayo wiped his tears of laughter from his eye with a curled finger. "You must really have ya family fooled with this school teacher act. Come on, I know ya had some sort of clue, doll face." he nudged her head with his gun. Monica narrowed her eyelids into slits, peering at her husband not believing that he had lied to her for all of the years that they had been together.

"Yes, It's true..." he casted his eyes down at the floor shamefully. He never wanted his family to find out what he really did for a living. More importantly, he didn't want his profession to come back and haunt his loved ones. But this did happen, and now it was too late. "I've been a contract killer for the past fifteen years." he looked up at his wife with tearing eyes. "I'm sorry, baybe."

All Monica could do was cry and stare at the man that she thought she knew better than herself. She was shocked and heartbroken at the same damn time. She couldn't worry about that at this minute though because her and her son's lives hung in the balance.

"You told us dat chu took care of that padre, but we found out recently that he made it out to New Zealand which is where you helped him to get." Jayo looked at him pitifully.

"Big fuckin' mistake." the nigga standing to his left stated.

"How could you allow a man to live that has stolen the innocence of so many children?"

Julian didn't say anything, he was too busy wallowing in self pity.

"You hear me talking to you, bruvh, huh?"

"He swore to God that he didn't do it, that Tiny wanting him dead was behind an entirely different reason."

"And you fell for that bullshit?" Jayo gritted as he talked, pupils raging with fire. "Knowing that you're so fucking gullible makes me completely justified in doing this." Pop! Monica's head jerked violently and half of her face went flying across the living room. Smoke rose from the back of her head and her eyes rolled over to their whites, as she went flying toward her son's lap. J.J's eyes snapped open and he wailed at the top of his lungs, seeing the gaping bloody hole at the back of his mother's skull. His father was mortified seeing his wife get her mothafucking wig split right before his tearing eyes. He went to rush the gunman but his men drew down on him, stopping him dead in his tracks. Right there in the middle of the floor, he bawled his eyes out, sinking his fingers into the carpet. His

tears fell in abundance and he hollered out, the sound of his voice syncing in and out.

"Ya bloody black hearted bastard, ya dead! Ya hear me, ya muddafucka?" he bellowed, turning red in the face. The veins in his temples and neck pulsated. "You're so mudafucking dead!"

Jayo stepped to the back of J.J, pressing that cold metal to the back of his dome. He smiled fiendishly, his threatening eyes leaped back and forth between Julian and his young son. The little nigga squeezed his eyelids shut and whimpered, snot dripping out of his nose. His tears slicked his cheeks and dripped on his T-shirt.

"Noooooooooo," Julian scrambled upon his feet, trying to get to the mad man with the gun before he was able to give his son that eternal sleep.

Pop!

J.J slumped forward having a bullet put into the back of his skull. He sat hunched over his dead mother; smoke rose in the air from the back of his dome piece. By this time his father was on his feet making hurried steps towards Jayo with tears cascading down his cheeks. The vengeful man lifted his gun and pulled the trigger. The weapon bucked in his hand and splattered a hole in Julian's chest, whipping his head back. He went falling back towards to the floor awkwardly, but not before taking two more shots with him on the way down. Jayo and his men came from behind the couch. He stopped to give the family man the once over to make sure that he was dead before leaving the house as quietly as he came.

"Uhhhhhh," Julian moaned and blinked his eyelids. He was seeing through blurred vision being that he was losing so much blood. Looking over his shoulder, he made an ugly face seeing his family had been murdered in cold

blood. "My baybe...my son." he cried and sniffled, then his head bobbled. He was feeling woozy from all of his bleeding. He moved about lazily trying to locate the telephone. Spotting it at the far corner of the room, he pulled himself up by the curtain and staggered over to the telephone. His crimson stained hand picked up the receiver and dialed 9-1-1. Once he'd finished his call, he staggered over to the couch where his family was laid out and plopped down beside them. He kissed them both on their heads and lay back on the couch, leaking. He felt his eyelids getting heavier and heavier, and right when he was about to shut them, the paramedics came bursting through the door alongside the police.

Julian eventually recovered from his wounds at the hospital. From there he went on to murder out Jayo and his men, claiming his vengeance and putting his family's souls to rest. Once his loved ones were in the ground, he vowed to fulfill every contract that he came across and to be as cold as a glass of ice water when it came to the business of murder.

Present

"Mr. King...Mr. King!" Annabella said louder and louder until the killer's head snapped up. He'd been recalling the day that his family had been slaughtered in front of him while he twisted his wedding band around his finger, back and forth.

He stopped twisting his ring around his finger and sat up in the chair, clearing his throat with a fist to his mouth.

"Yes."

"I'm terribly sorry for your loss."

"As I am of yours."

Suddenly, his cell phone rang and vibrated. He pulled it out of his jacket and checked the display, wearing a plain expression on his face. His eyes shifted up from the cellular's screen and landed on his employer's. "This is da man dat's gonna place your father's murderer right into my lap. Excuse me, gimmie one minute." he threw up a finger and rose from out of the chair. He dipped off to the corner of the office away from her eavesdropping ears and held a quick conversation before disconnecting the call. Sliding the device back inside of his jacket, he stepped back before the desk.

"I hope that was good news."

"Very good news." he assured her.

"Great." she stood to her feet, adjusting her skirt on her curvaceous hips. Next, she extended her manicured hand and said, "I guess I'll see you very soon."

"Count onnit, Ms. Bemmy," he gave her a firm handshake and made his departure.

CHaPtER OnE

Rio de Janeiro, Brazil

Fear's eyes snapped open and he stared up at the ceiling for a while. He'd grown a thick crop of hair which he wore in a bun and a beard so full and long it tickled his chest. He was as naked as the day he was snatched out of his mother's womb. Lying in bed on both sides of him was last night's entertainment, two of the most beautiful Brazilian whores he'd ever have the privilege of laying eyes on. Fear slid out of bed and poured himself a glass of Tequila. He took the bottle to the head, drinking the last of the alcohol it had left and swallowing the worm that was held prisoner inside. He took a sip from his glass and headed over to the small table and chair in the corner, cock swing from left to right. He moved around the room like a nigga that was fully clothed. He reached inside of the breast pocket of his plaid shirt that was hanging onto the back of the chair. When his hand came back up it was holding a picture of him and Anton. They were standing back to back holding guns and making tough faces.

He took a sip of his drink as he stared down at the picture. "I'll be waiting."

Seven years ago Fear was hired to carry out a contract on a man by the name of Bootsy Jackson. The hit was paid for by the victim's own wife, Giselle Jackson. When the killer handled this execution he had no idea that years later he would eventually meet their children, Eureka and Anton. He unexpectedly fell in love with their daughter and developed a brotherhood with their son. The guilt of having killed their father ate away at his soul and the day that he was about to reveal his sin to them, Eureka uncovered his secret. At the time Fear was designated to

12

capture or kill Eureka by a drug dealer by the name of Malvo. The hit-man made good on his end of the deal and walked away one hundred thousand dollars richer, but not before freeing Eureka of her bondages. Having been let loose, Eureka snatched up a Machete to send Malvo to the afterlife. But before she could break the sixth commandment the Russian mafia and the Greek mafia showed up looking forward to having the drug dealer's blood on their hands. It turns out that the drug dealer owed both families a shit load of money. Eureka gave him up in order for her to walk away unscathed. It was then left up to the two mob crews to decide what they were going to do with Malvo. They settled on killing him together. That was the only way they felt like justice could be served between the two of them. With Eureka and Anton out of harm's way, Fear took it upon himself to flee Los Angeles. He didn't want to spend the rest of his life there being haunted by the evil he had done so he figured that it would be best that he took up time somewhere else, Brazil. Now here he was living like a king in one of the world's most beautiful cities.

The sudden ringing and vibrating of his cellular stole his attention and caused the women in his bed to stir. Tossing the picture down on the tabletop, he hurried over to the nightstand. He picked up his cell phone and plopped down on the bed. Once he looked at the screen and saw *Nero* he cracked a slight smile. Anytime he saw this name on the display it meant a payday for him. See, he worked for him exclusively and he paid handsomely. Not to mention, there was chances of some action, which was right up the killer's alley since he hadn't been on a mission in quite some time. It wasn't necessarily the money that he was looking forward to, but the thrill of being in the thick of things. He missed that almost as much as he missed Eureka and Anton.

"Boss dawg, what's up with it?" Fear spoke into the cell phone. He then switched hands with cellular and picked up his boxer briefs, slipping them on.

"I gotta job for you."

"Is that right? What chu got for me to get into?"

"Meet me at the club."

"Alright," he picked his watch up off of the nightstand to read the time, "Gimme like half an hour."

Fear disconnected the call and got dressed, tucking his gun in the small of his back. Snatching the keys off of the table, he hurried out of the house and hustled down the steps, jumping down to the ground. He ran over to a sky blue F-150 Ford pickup truck with a rusted driver side door. Once he slid in behind the wheel, he resurrected the vehicle's engine. The old heap kicked twice, exhaust pipe fluttering smoke before it started up. After he threw the gear in reverse, he threw his arm over the headrest and looked out of the back window. He mashed the gas pedal and the truck went flying backwards, kicking up debris. The pickup swung around and he went speeding off in the opposite direction. Fear gripped the steering wheel with one hand while his head was on a constant swivel. He took in the scenery of Rio's ghetto through the dirt speckled windshield. The ground was nothing more than paved dirt while the homes were made of mixed match shudders. There were teenagers hanging out getting drunk and slap boxing while the younger kids played soccer out in the middle of the road. Fear grinned seeing the children chuckling and laughing as they kicked the ball around. He honked the horn as he came upon them. Their heads snapped in his direction and they broke into wide smiles, eyes lighting up when they saw him. "Fear, Fear, Fear," they called out his name and came running. The kid that owned the ball snatched it up and came hurrying along with the rest of the kids. All of the children came crowding the driver side window of the pickup. Some of their hair was wild and unkempt, while their clothing either didn't match or was wrinkled. Nonetheless, they were all very excited to see him. You would have thought that he was a celebrity or some shit.

"Aye, what's up?" the boy with the ball held out his fist.

"What it do, lil' homie?" he touched fists with him, as well as the rest of the little dudes present.

"What's up, Fear? What's up, big homie? What it do?"

The youngsters sounded off all at once.

"Can we ride with you?" the boy with the ball inquired.

"I got some moves I gotta make right now, family, maybe later on." he gave him something to look forward to.

"You still gon' tell me how to drive?"

"Yep, I gave you my word and a man always…"

"…Keeps his word!" the children spoke in unison, finishing what he was saying.

"That's right," he glanced at the time on his cellular, seeing that it was almost time for him to meet up with old boy. "Check it y'all. I gotta cut this short, but I'll get up with y'all later. Until then, y'all have y'all selves some ice cream on me." he pulled a wad of money out of his cargo pants, holding it in one hand and using the other to count how many kids there was in all. Once he calculated, he counted off the number of bills he needed and passed them out of the window to the youngster with the soccer ball. His youthful eyes became as big as silver dollars when the dead presidents touched his hands. "Wow!" his face lit up, staring at all of that money in his possession. "Thanks, Fear."

"You're welcome, lil' homie." he watched as all of the kids surrounded the boy with the money in frenzy, swallowing him up. It looked like one thousand hands were reaching trying to get the bills. The noise that they were making sounded like there was a riot taking place in the streets. Fear smiled happily and threw his pickup into drive, taking off down the road.

Sometime later Fear brought the old pickup truck just outside a bar in the richer area of the city. Right when he was turning off the engine, some drunken bastard was getting thrown out on his ass by a blob of a man that he assumed was the bouncer of the joint. He wore a bald head and a flabby body that donned a sleeveless jean jacket with white fur around the collar and boots.

"And stay out!" he shouted out to the lush he'd thrown from out of the establishment, showcasing the lone rotten tooth in his mouth. Next, he brushed the imaginary dirt from his hands. He made to go back inside but stopped in his tracks once he saw Fear stashing his keys inside of his pocket as he rounded his truck. Immediately, he turned back around, blocking the doorway and folding his arms across his hairy chest, mad dogging him.

Fear looked at the lush slowly scrambling to his feet having been thrown out of the bar. Over his shoulder he could hear the crunked up music as well as the hoots and hollers of men that were being entertained by half naked and fully nude women. When he turned back around he saw flickers of the action taking place inside behind the brute

16

that was guarding the door. He could tell by the expression on his face that he was going to bust his balls before allowing him inside. This was something that he was far from being ready to deal with. All he wanted to do was see what that nigga Nero wanted and get the hell up from out of there. As easy as it sounded inside of his head he knew that it wasn't going to be as simple. He didn't know if it was because he was such a short man, or if he just looked like the type that could be pushed over, but he was always running into some asshole that wanted to give him a hard time lately. Taking a deep breath, Fear stepped to the man at the entrance sizing him up.

"You want access? It's ten bucks entree fee, plus a two drink minimum." The giant said.

"I'm here to see Nero." Fear told him with a no nonsense attitude.

"I don't care if you're here to see the goddamn pope," he jabbed him in the chest with his stubby finger, raining spittle in his face as he barked on him, "It's still ten bucks to enter, plus a two drink minimum!" He clenched his jaws and breathed heavily, his nostrils flaring and blowing hot air into his face. Fear looked down at his finger which was buried into the fabric of his shirt. His eyes studied it as if it were a ketchup stain on a fresh white T-shirt. He squared his jaws and they pulsated. Looking back up at the blob, he grabbed his finger and snapped it to the right, breaking it. His big ass howled like a wounded dog, before he was kicked in the balls. The explosion of pain caused his eyes to double to the size of golf balls. When he grabbed his precious stones with his good hand, he was rewarded with a kick in the chin. The impact from the blow flipped him over onto his round belly and sent him sliding inside of the shitty bar, eventually turning over on his back.

17

It was like the patrons inside didn't notice him how they went on about their dealings like a four hundred pound man was lying dead smack in the middle of the floor. Fear came strolling inside of the place tossing ten wrinkled dollar bills onto the big man's belly. One of the bills fell loose from the others and slid beneath his triple chin. His eyes were narrowed into slits and he made noises like a pig, knocked the fuck out.

Fear took in the establishment with a keen eye. The place was that big, but from all of the noise it made outside it could have easily been thought to be much bigger. There were niggaz sitting at the scattered tables drinking mugs of beer and watching the show that a curvaceous, copper skinned goddess put on with a python around her neck, while the others were preoccupied with a lady or two of their very own dancing provocatively for them. The other patrons played the bar egging the entertainment on, shooting the shit and/or trying to talk one of the girls into dip off with them for a private show.

Fear set his sights on the bartender who had just popped the caps off of two Coronas and set them before two patrons that were laughing their asses off at something or another. Focused, he stepped onto the blobs belly without breaking his stride. When he made it to the bar he motioned the bartender over and he leaned forward to hear what he wanted to order over the loud music.

"I was told that you have a two drink minimum here. Is that right?"

"Correct."

"Alright, I want two shots of Patron'."

"Comin' right up," he set out two shot glasses and placed a slice of lime on each of their respective rims.

He then whipped out the bottle and began filling up the glasses.

"Do me a favor, uhhh," he searched his vest for a name tag, pointing his finger and peering closely.

"Hector." he glanced up from the glasses as he filled them.

"Hector, tell my good friend Nero that Fear's here to see 'em."

"Gotcha."

"This here," he held up a fifty dollar bill then placed it on the bar top, sitting a half empty Corona bottle on top of it, "is for you."

"Thank you." he nodded and glanced over his shoulder, worry etched across his face. "Uh, Fear, right?"

"That's right," he pinched the shot glass between his fingers and threw it back, hissing.

"Jumbo's comin'." he leaned closer and whispered.

"Would that be the large gentleman I had the pleasure of meeting before entering this fine establishment?" he pinched the second shot glass between his fingers and brought it to his lips.

"Yes."

"I know." Through the corner of his eye, Fear could see Jumbo stalking toward him. Niggaz and bitchez were getting the fuck up outta his way, zipping back and forth across him. "Let me worry about the fat man. You just do me a favor and get boss dawg for me."

"Alright." he nodded, pressing the red button underneath the ledge of the bar top.

"I'm gonna cutta Chinese letter into ya face…" Jumbo unsheathed the knife from off of his hip. Once the light hit it a gleam swept up the length of its jagged blade. Its metal was so shiny that it resembled silver. The blob lifted his knife above his head and swung it downward at his enemy's skull. At the last minute Fear jumped backwards and swung around, pulling his .9mm from his back. He turned his banger on the raging man, whom looked surprised that he was able to move so swiftly.

Bloc! Bloc!

He blew holes into both of his kneecaps, dropping him down to the scuffed hardwood floor. He hollered out with tears dancing in his eyes, bleeding out on the surface. Having dropped his knife, he looked around for it. When he spotted it he went to pick it up and it was shot out of his grasp, a spark flying from off it. Gritting, he turned his hateful eyes on the gunman. Fear tossed back his last shot of Patron and smacked the glass down on the bar top, wiping his mouth with his fist. The music had stopped and everyone inside of the club had frozen where they stood watching the little man with the gun and anticipating what he would do next.

Fear approached Jumbo and placed his gun at the center of his forehead, its hot barrel sizzled his skin. The big man winced feeling the burning against his flesh.

"Look at me," he spoke with a seriousness that dripped like rain from his vocal cords. "Look. At. Me..." he said louder, gauging him to peel his eyelids open. When he did tears threatened to spill down his cheeks. "You fucked with the wrong one." he snarled and went to pull the trigger.

"Fear!" a voice boomed from his rear, pausing his pulling of the trigger. Behind him at the top of the staircase was Nero.

Fear didn't have to turn around to know that it was the man that had requested him, but that didn't make him divide his attention. Nah, the fat mothafucka at his knees had his sole attention.

"Consider yourself lucky, family, 'cause normally whomever's on the opposite end of my banger is as good as dead." he took the steel away from his forehead then whacked him upside his dome with it. Jumbo slammed the side of his head against the floor, lying awkwardly with one leg underneath him. Fear tucked his burner on his waistline and turned around to Nero, spreading his arms and smiling. It was crazy how he was just mad dogging Jumbo, but now he was cheesing like he was about to take a picture. "Nero, my nigga, what's up with it?"

Just then he heard a stampede of footsteps coming up behind him. When he turned around there was a bunch of badges filling up the entrance of the establishment. For most this would have been caused to be alarmed, but not for Fear. He was familiar with all of these crooked ass mothafuckaz; Nero had every last one of them in pocket. The leader of their pack looked up at the Brazilian crime boss and he gave him a nod, letting him know that everything was okay. With that signal given, he tucked his gun inside of its holster and so did his men. He told them something in their native language and they made their exit.

"Come on up." Nero motioned for Fear to come up the steps with a sway of his cane. As he waited for his guest to join him, his eyes took a tour of his business. The atmosphere was void of sound given that the music had been turned off and all of the patrons' eyes were on him. "Cut the music back on goddamn it, we've got people here tryna have a good time and you're fucking it up!" With that being said, the music was cut back on and the patrons went back to their business like none of that shit had just gone down. When Fear past Nero he patted his back and looked out on the floor, seeing two of his men pulling Jumbo upon his feet and dragging him off on his knees. This left twin blood smears on the floor. The bartender hopped over the bar with a single handed leap and retrieved a mop. He didn't waste any time going about the task of cleaning the mess up.

Nero stepped inside of his office shutting the door behind him. He found Fear standing at the chair at his desk, looking around at the decor as he waiting for him. The digs in the place was very simple. He had a shiny, oak wood desk, a black leather executive chair, a "42 flat-screen on the far wall and two black leather and suede couches with a coffee table sitting at the center. The space looked like a doctor's office.

"Please, have a seat." Nero motioned toward the chair that his guest was standing at the back of. Fear pulled out his banger and sat down on the chair, placing it on the desktop. He noticed Nero looking a little uneasy and he wanted to put his mind at ease.

"Don't mind me; I just don't want her digging into my back. As a matter of fact," he picked the handgun up and ejecting the magazine. He cocked it back and the bullet shot up into the air spinning around in circles, looking like a copper blur. He snatched it out of the air and smacked it down on the desktop along with the magazine. "There, is that better?" he cracked a grin.

"Yes." Nero replied, sitting behind the desk and sitting his cane aside. "You'll have to excuse my paranoia, but with as many assassination attempts that I've had on my life, could ju blame me?" he unfastened the button on his suit's jacket, and for the first time the killer saw the imprint of the bulletproof vest that he was sporting beneath his button-down shirt.

Fear wasn't insulted that the Brazilian crime boss was skeptical of him. Honestly, he couldn't blame the old man. He was the most powerful gangster in that country. Nothing illegal could be moved and no one could be murdered unless he gave the okay for it. He got fifty cents on every dollar that was made or the nigga that chose to buck got laid down with some hot shit. There were no negotiations and no one was above his law. That's just how the fuck it was, plain and simple. This was the reason that every thug, criminal, and two bit hustler wanted him dead. They knew that if they could get him out of the way then they could see more profit than they did with him alive. This is why these individuals set aside their differences and united to put together their money to hire an assassin. Everything was set in place and Nero was sure as hell supposed to have died that day, but there was one thing that the trigger man didn't count on...Fearless.

Fear had been living like a king since taking up in Rio. Although he had to kick up half to Nero as a rule when entered the city, he still had fifty thousand dollars left, which was more than enough for him to live like royalty down there. Still, eventually the money he had stashed away would dry up one day so he had to find himself some employment quick. An honest job definitely wasn't going to cover the expenses of the lifestyle that he was accustomed to, so he had to get his out of the mud like the rest of the criminals out there. He was working as an enforcer for this local crew, but the change they were breaking him off was worth far less his expertise. With that in mind, he stopped fucking with them niggaz and just started robbing them blind. This nigga got on his Omar from *The Wire* shit, banging hammers and pumping his namesake into fools' hearts. Niggaz started operating under the radar so his victims came few and far in between. One day he found himself sitting on ten stacks. That's when he realized that he had to hit him a lick and he had to hit him one fast, if he planned on eating.

Flashback

Fear had come walking out of the store with groceries when he saw Nero and his bodyguard emerge from out of the barber shop. The two men were en route towards the stretch Benz limousine that was waiting at the curb idling. Nero tipped the brim of his hat to the killer remembering having met him when he had to split his loot when he entered the country. Fear gave him a nod and bit into the peach that he'd just taken out of his grocery bag. A line formed across his forehead seeing the florescent light shining on the Brazilian crime boss's face. He was about to take another bite out of his peach when he noticed where the light was reflecting from. He followed the light and found someone in the window with the rifle aimed at Nero.

Fear had just taken a bite out of the peach when he noticed him. He spat out the part of the fruit that he chewed and dropped his bag of groceries. Everything seemed to be moving in slow motion when he shouted a warning out to Nero and his bodyguard, making hurried steps in their direction. He pointed up to the window while en route. Seeing him do this, the bodyguard drew iron and went to spit heat at the sniper. He was far too late though. The sniper was faster than he was on the trigger. A single shot made the top of his skull come loose and sent his brains flying everywhere. By this time Fear was drawing his gun and leaping into the air. He tackled Nero to the sidewalk and rolled off of him. The crime boss scrambled away like a wounded dog and took cover. Once Fear saw that Nero was safe and sound, he came back up with his gun spitting hot fire. The weapon reclined with the first shot it fired and empty shell casings came flying out. The bullet whizzed through the air and shattered the scope of the assassin's sniper rifle exiting the back of his skull. He staggered back from the window like a zombie. Fear rose to his booted feet, approaching and firing his burner. Slugs blew through the window's glass and pelted the mothafucka'z body that they were meant for until he dropped to the floor dead, expelling his last breath.

Fear lowered the hand that held the gun to his side, staring up at the broken out window breathing heavily. Figuring that he had successfully murdered the sniper, he checked the magazine of his gun and saw that he had emptied half of the rounds it contained. He smacked the magazine into the butt of the weapon and started over to Nero who was ducked down behind his stretch Benz a little shaken up; being that his life was almost stolen from him. When Nero looked to his right and saw a shadow approaching, he was about to take off running until he realized that it was the man that had tackled him to the ground from the sniper's bullet. The foreigner rounded the rear of the vehicle and stopped before him. The Brazilian crime boss took him in from his boots to his head. The sun shined at the back of him keeping his face in darkness but the silhouette of his dreads were visible as he extended his hand. Nero stared at it for a time trying to make heads or tails of the situation. For all he knew this could be a trick and this man could have been sent to collect a bounty on his head. Shaking the thought from his mental, he grasped the stranger's hand and allowed him to pull him to his feet.

"Thank you."

Fear gave him a nod.

From that day forth Fear was under Nero's employ.
He sent him to kill niggaz that didn't come up off of what
they owed him and to collect his taxes. For his services he
was given paradise in the beautiful city.

Present

"Soooo, who's program do you need me to get
with?" Fear got right down to business. Anytime the OG
called upon him he knew that it was time for some gunplay
which was fine by him being that meant he was going to
eat.

Nero pulled open his desk drawer and removed
several photographs, tossing them onto the desktop before
him. The first two photos slid from beneath one another
from the impact. Fear picked the photos up and looked
through them. They were all photos of Raymar at different
locations as well as one mug shot.

"He's a snitch," Nero informed him.

Fear's eyes shifted up from the photographs, locking
eyes with his employer's. "I fucking hate rats. When you
need this nigga'z obituary?"

"He's my son."

"Son?" his brows furrowed.

"Yes...my son." he said with an unfortunate
expression on his face. He was ashamed to share the same
bloodline as a nigga that ratted. And although he wanted to
do nothing more than throw his offspring to the wolves, he
was his father. And all parents wanted to protect their
children no matter what bad they'd done. That's just how it
was.

Raymar wanted to prove to his father that he had
what it took to stand shoulder to shoulder with the criminals
of his father's organization. He thought it was no better way

26

than for him to execute a job and show his old man that he was worthy to sit at a table with his crew. Having made up his mind Raymar and a few connected guys decided to pull a diamond heist worth $100,000,000 dollars. Once the caper was done it was Raymar's duty to dispose of the weapons, equipment, and van used for the task. On his way to do just that he got pulled over by the cops and found himself down at 77 division precinct being interrogated. Needless to say, he folded like a lawn chair and told on everybody and their baby's daddy. Less than eight hours later his crime partners' doors were being kicked down and they were being handcuffed. When it was all said and done, those niggaz got hit with thirty years apiece, while Raymar, the mastermind of the entire hit, got a measly five years for his cooperation with the feds.

Fear tossed the photos back upon the desktop and sat back in his chair, steepling his hands in his lap. "So, what's up? You want me to do junior in?"

"No. I pulled some string to have him transported to another prison." he filled him in. "At this location I have a little more juice, but I don't know how long I can keep the dogs from tearing into him. That's where you come in." he took the time to clip off the end of a thick ass cigar and lit it up, tossing the Zippo lighter upon the desktop. He blew a cloud of smoke up into air. It wafted around making it appear as if he manifested out of it.

"Exactly where do I fit in this equation if you don't want junior here whacked?" he inquired with a confused look upon his face, narrowing his eyelids.

"I want chu to recover him and bring him back here to me; to Brazil. I'm confident that I can protect him here."

"That's a tall order, Boss Dawg." he sat up in his chair once he realized he was as serious as cancer about the stunt that he wanted him to lie down.

"I know. You don't think you can do it?"

"Shiiiet, if I can't do it then it can't be done." he spoke arrogantly, staring him dead in his eyes.

"Then you'll bring Ray back here to me?" he said with hopeful eyes.

"Safe and sound, but how much is he worth to you?"

"Five hundred thousand dollars."

"Family, you've got yourself a deal." he shot to his feet and extended his hand. Nero got upon his feet and grasped it, giving him a firm shake.

Fear was whisked from the bar and taken straight to the airport. As soon as he landed in Los Angeles he was picked up in a Lincoln Town Car and taken to an auto body garage. It was there that he was given an armored Mustang sports car, a suit of body armor and a shotgun amongst other things.

****

Raymar stood in line amongst several other inmates shackled the fuck up and waiting to board the prison bus that would bring him to his destination. He appeared to be a nervous wreck, looking all around him and suspecting someone to come out the blue to shank him. A few days ago a crooked CO had given him a contraband cell phone and told him that there was one telephone number listed as a contact. This number belonged to his father. He was given strict orders to contact him as soon as possible. Raymar did exactly what he was told. His old man assured him that he was going to be alright because he had come up with something to get him out of his situation. He sighed with relief hearing that he was going to get transported from out of the prison where everybody and their baby momma was gunning for him for what he had done. Calmness came over him knowing that at Corcoran there would be niggaz there that would watch his back. Now all he had to do was make it there in one piece.

Once all of the inmates were accounted for and had boarded the bus, a CO came down alongside it with a long black metal rod that curved at its end. Attached to it was a small rectangle mirror. He stuck it just underneath the transporting vehicle and walked alongside both ends of it, making sure there wasn't anything that threatened the passenger's safety. Once this was done, he radioed the driver and he cranked that big bastard of a bus up. Having checked his entire mirror, he pulled off and headed for the barbed wired gates.

The convicts were on their way to their new home.

****

Vrooooooom!

The Mustang's engine whined as it shot up the road leaving debris up in the air. Its limousine tinted windows and dull black paint made it look like an electric shaver. It swept up beside the prison bus, rolling beside it for a time, allowing the inmates aboard to take a gander at the finely tuned machine. Its appearance caused a ruckus inside. Grown ass men were acting like children at a zoo, oohing and awing behind the gated windows of the transporting bus. Abruptly, the Mustang swerved in front of the bus, zooming a safe distance ahead. Beneath the vehicle slots opened on either side of it and small metal spiked balls were released. They tumbled down the road like loose oranges en route towards the bus. *Boof! Boof!* The tires sounded off one after the next and then there was an *Urkkkkkkk!* The driver struggled with control of the enormous vehicle. He swerved left and then right, but eventually it flipped over, tumbling a short distance and sliding down the asphalt. It came to a stop, lying still with its wreckage on either sides of it, smoke emitting from it.

Scurrrrr!

The Mustang made the noise as its driver whipped it around, shifting gears and pulling the emergency brake up. When it came to a complete stop it was facing the prison bus. It zipped back up the road and skidded to a stop beside the bus. The driver side door was thrown open and out stepped a short man wearing a gas mask, helmet, and a body of armor. He racked his shotgun and kicked the cracked window of the bus until the glass gave. Next, he pulled the pins from two gas grenades and tossed them inside the transporting vehicle. He watched as the inmates and guards gagged and choked on the yellowish gas that was spraying from the grenades. He stole a glance at his digital watch and then looked inside of the bus. Everyone had slowly started to fall out like dead roaches. Figuring that he'd best make his move now, he made his way inside, shotgun at the ready in case anyone gave him trouble. Taking a hold of his bolt-cutters, he cut the shackles from Raymar's wrists and ankles. He then smacked his gas mask over the lower half of his face and gave him instructions to hold it in place, as the young man gagged and coughed.

"Watch out!" Raymar's eyes snapped open and he pointed ahead. The short man whipped around to see a nauseated guard lifting his gun but before he could pull the trigger he got a chest full of some hot shit. The report from the shotgun lifted him off of his steel toe leather boots and dropped him on his ass. The short man whipped his shotgun around the bus, looking for anyone else that may try him but they were all out cold. He grabbed Raymar roughly by his arm and hurriedly escorted him towards the exit. As soon as he stepped a boot out on the broken glass littered surface assault rifle fire woke up the day.

Ratatatatatatatatat!

Ping! Ting! Ziiiiiing!

Sparks flew off the side of the bus and nearly took off the short man's head. He pulled Raymar along and they ducked for cover in front of the bus. Clutching his shotgun and holding up against his chest, he peeked around the corner of the bus to see who it was trying to knock his wig off. He made a jet black nigga rocking cornrows and hanging out of the driver side window of a Dodge Durango with an AK-47.

"Stay here." The short man commanded Raymar before swinging out from behind the front of the bus, shotgun braced against his shoulder. He shut one eyelid and took aim, pulling the trigger. The powerful weapon jerked with each blast it released.

Bloom! Bloom! Bloom!

The short man let his shotgun rip at the oncoming Dodge Durango cracking its windshield and blowing out one of the front tires. The truck swerved out of control and flipped over twice, skidding on its rooftop until it eventually stopped.

The gunner groaned as he slowly crawled out of the wrecked SUV slicing up his hands. His face was bloody and littered with cuts from the broken glass. He blinked his right eyelid repeatedly trying to stop the blood from getting in it. He looked up ahead through blurred vision seeing the nigga that had blasted on him and the man he'd come to execute. As fast as he could he pulled out his cellular and zoomed in on the gunman's face, snapping several pictures of him. He then sent them to the number stored inside of his contact,

Frost. This was the last thing he did before his head smacked down on the pavement. Lying on the ground wide eyed, he unleashed his last breath.

The short man threw Raymar into the front passenger seat and slammed the door closed. He fired up the Mustang and floored it, tires squealing as he left skid marks on the road.

Raymar pulled off the gasmask, looking from the man that had stolen him and over his shoulder at the ruined prison bus which was growing smaller and smaller the further they drove.

"Hey, thanks, thanks a lot," he said to the man. The man took a gander at his charge but set his eyes back on the road. "I take it my father sent chu, that's a no brainer." The man twisted his lips and looked at him like *Why don't you shut the fuck up?* "My dad did send you for me, didn't he?" he asked, a little scared this time. His heart thumped as he moved his hand toward the door's handle.

"Yeah, your dad sent me." Fear responded with annoyance.

"Oh thank God." he sighed with relief, leaning his head back against the headrest and taking a deep breath. He lifted his head and looked to his rescuer. "I thought you were one of them."

"You mean the mothafuckaz that chu snitched on peoples?" his eyebrows arched. "Nah, I'm not one of them. But had they hired me yo' ass would have already been dead, best believe that."

Raymar was quiet for a moment realizing the man wasn't snitch friendly. He changed the subject. "Hey, man, I'm Raymar, but my friends call me, Ray." He extended his hand and the man looked at it like he'd just used it to scratch his ass.

The man fished around inside of the ashtray until he found a roach of a blunt. He stuck it in his mouth and ripped a match stick from out of a book. He swiped it across the lower half of his charge's stubble face causing him to grimace. He then used it to light up his blunt, fanning out its flame and tossing it out of the window. Raymar winced as he flipped the sun-visor down and looked in the mirror, turning his face to the side. There was a pink streak there where the match had been swept across.

The man sucked on the end of roach causing smoke to emit. He took it from his mouth and gave him his name, "Fear. Now, shut the fuck up talking to me. I hate rats. As a matter of fact, nigga, take a nap." He cracked him in the chin, knocking him unconscious. Looking from the road to what he was doing, he let the front passenger seat back. He then went about smoking his L and occasionally glancing at the picture of Anton, Eureka and him in the dashboard.

"Damn, a nigga miss y'all, man."

Chapter 2
That night

His fists looked like blurs as he worked the speed bag, eyes focused, forehead beaded with sweat. Although he was beating on the bag, he envisioned himself breaking his father's killer off something real proper like. The funny thing was his opponent was the hardest one he'd faced yet and their scrapping was one of the toughest brawls he'd ever experienced in his life.

He knew the day would come that they would lock ass and he wanted to be especially prepared for that date.

After Fear's disappearance, Anton picked up exactly where he'd left off. He got contracts from the likes of some of the most powerful and influential men around the world. They paid handsomely which allowed him to take good care of his family and move into the enormous mansion he was in. With all of the money he'd made, he could have easily fell back from the murder game but it was something about the thrill of the hunt that kept his heart beating. He didn't see himself turning his back on the game anytime soon. Far as he was concerned, he was going to ride it out until he saw a 6 x 9 or a grave.

Bunk! Bunk! Bunk! Bunk! Bunk!

Anton jabbed the speed bag one last time before drying off with the white towel and unwrapping his fists. He was now twenty years old and had changed considerably since he was fifteen. He stood five foot ten and sported an athletic physique. Over the years he'd grown in knowledge, wisdom and strength.

Buzzzzzzz!

He hung his towel around his neck and approached the intercom. He held down the button. "What's up, sis?"

"Dinners ready, baby boy." Eureka responded.

He held the button down. "Alright, I'ma shower and head on up."

"See ya then."

After hitting the shower which was located at the back of the gym, Anton got dressed in a throwback Chicago Bulls jersey Michael Jordan 23, gray sweats and a pair of 13s. He took the elevator upstairs and walked across the enormous living room en route to the kitchen. On his way there, he could smell the delicious meal his sister prepared. As soon as he crossed the threshold into the kitchen, he was greeted by their little addition.

"Uncle Ant, where you been?" The brown skinned three year old sitting at the table asked. Eureka had just sat a plate of lasagna, garlic bread and Caesar salad before him. "I've been looking all over for you?"

Anton cracked a smile. "I was down in the gym, chump, waiting on you. You must of gotten scared I was gon' whip your butt." He threw phantom punches at the kid and he hopped up out of his chair, swinging back. He laughed and giggled as he tried his best to put hands on his uncle. The little guy was quite nice with his hands. This was because Anton would get up every morning and train him down in the gym. He was teaching him other things as well, but they kept that between them because if the boy's mother was to ever find out she'd wring her baby brother's neck.

Anton amused his nephew bobbing and weaving his punches, all the while watching his foot work. He was pleased to see he had picked up the skills he'd taught and he was confident one day he'd find out if he remembered his other lessons as well.

Eureka smiled looking at the most important men in her life playing around. She sat Anton's plate and his glass

35

of juice down on the table and folded her arms across her chest, watching them.

Little man swung and Anton faked like he had connected with his chin, falling out on the floor. Seeing this, his nephew shadowboxed and showed off his footwork, as if he'd really put in some work on his opponent.

"Reka," Anton whispered with one eye open, getting his sister's attention.

"Yeah?" she whispered back.

"Start the count."

"Oh, sure thing."

Anton closed both of his eyelids pretending to be knocked out. She stood over him counting while her offspring continued with his shadowboxing. Once she was done, she held up her son's arm. "And the winner by knockout ladies and gentlemen, Kingston 'Steel Hands' Jackson."

Kingston stood there smiling as his mother and uncle made sounds of a crowd roaring in excitement.

40 minutes later

The Jacksons had eaten and chatted after. Everyone was good and full.

Kingston and Eureka were laughing at Anton's telling of a funny story when the little boy noticed his uncle's hand. The sight of it made his forehead wrinkle a bit.

"Uncle Ant."

Anton came down from his laughter. "What's up, my man?"

"How'd you get those scars?" he asked curiously.

Anton looked at his hand. It bared missing knuckles, scars, and burn marks. He made his hand into a fist and sat it down on the table top.

"Surviving, I fight to survive."

"Why do you survive?"

"So I can live and be able to take care of my family."

"Who's fam?"

"You and your mother." His motioned a finger between them.

"Oh," he said, picking up his glass of juice and taking a drink.

Eureka and Anton exchanged glances smiling.

She looked at her watch and frowned. "It's getting late. I needed to get him in the tub."

"Alright, I'll take care of the dishes." Anton rose to his feet.

"Thanks." Eureka told him, taking Kingston's hand. "Come on, baby, let's get chu washed up and in bed."

She disappeared through the kitchen's door and he went on to wash the dishes. Once he was done, he dried his hands off, killed the light and headed out of the door.

****

The elevator stopped in a dimly lit underground bunker and the doors separated. There was a black on black H2 Hummer, a Cadillac Escalade truck, and a motorcycle. All of these vehicles were polished to a fine black and sitting on some pretty chrome thangs. The illumination from the lights in the ceiling caused the chrome and the paint on them to gleam. Anton cracked a grin as he walked past the motorcycle dragging his hand across its shiny handle bars. Out of all of his toys, the bike was his favorite and he drove it the most. Anton approached a control board that was lit up like the control panel on the space ship on Star Trek. Over it there was a screen showing all angles of his mansion in squares. He had the best in surveillance cameras and home security systems. If a nigga was caught sneaking on his premises, then that was his ass. Anton looked over the screen to make sure his estate was good. He then looked down a row of neon lit switches, flipping them on one by one.

Flipping on the switch shined light on something behind a display glass that stretched across the entire wall. Anton approached the display, looking through the glass as he walked the length of it. He walked past a bow-gun, a Katana, a shield, a shotgun, and a suit of body armor and a black mask with goggles and a breathing mask. A utility belt was around its waist. Attached to it on one side was a nightstick and on the other was a holstered automatic handgun. He stopped and admired the suit of armor. It was one of many he wore when duty called. Anton's hand caressed the glass as he admired the suit before he moved on. His eyes came across the book that Fear had them read to gain the knowledge of century's worth of assassins. Next, there was a wrinkled letter. This was the letter that was inside of the envelope the hit-man had stuck inside of his pocket when he slipped him something that knocked him out cold.

Anton read the letter for what seemed like the millionth time.

Little Brother if only you knew how hard it was for me to tell you this. Words cannot begin to explain the sorrow I feel or the way my heart bleeds just thinking of what I am about to reveal. Although it pains me, it is only right that I tell you the truth. I am the one that killed your father.

The letter then went on to explain his mother's involvement and how terribly sorry he was and how he wished he could take what had happened back.

Knowing you, I know you're in your feelings right now. And I can't say that I blame you, you've got every right to be. You can hate me as much as you want because I deserve it. And should the day come where hating me just isn't enough for you anymore then me and you can settle this man to man, killer to killer, student to teacher.

Fearless

Anton's face contorted to something demonic as he gritted his teeth and balled his fingers into fists. Veins spread up his neck and forehead as his head slightly shook. With a growl, he punched the glass with his fist causing it to crack like a spider's web. Blood seeped from his slice knuckles and ran into the crevasses of the broken glass.

"I'm coming for you," he said, nostrils widening and decreasing as his jaws swelled. He looked up to the ceiling, clenching his fists tightly and screaming.

"I'm commminggg for youuuuuuu!" His voice echoed and bounced off of the walls inside of the bunker.

Anton's cellular ringing and vibrating inside of his pocket stole his attention. Digging inside of his pocket he pulled it out and looked at the screen. It read Frost. He answered the call and pressed the cell to his ear.

"Watts up?" he focused on the letter that was sitting behind the glass. Pressing his hand against it, he swept his thumb up and down the glass admiringly. "Worth my while, huh? Alright, I'll be there in a hot one. Peace." He disconnected the call and stashed the device back inside of his pocket. He allowed his eyes to linger on the letter for a time longer. Next, he took a deep breath and ran off to get ready for his meeting.

****

Julian lay on his car with his back against the windshield. His eyelids were shut and his arms were folded across his chest. Twenty minutes had passed the agreed upon time that he was suppose to meet with his plug and now he was beginning to get irritated. Peeling his eyelids open, he glanced at his watch for what must have been the thousandth time. He shut his eyelids briefly and took a deep breath, pulling out his burnout cell phone. Swiftly, he dialed up the nigga that he was supposed to have met with. Once the cellular began its ringing, he went to press it to his ear but froze when he heard a vehicle driving up. Looking to his left, he narrowed his eyelids, straining his sight against the twin florescent orbs approaching him. Figuring that it must be his plug, he disconnected the call and stashed the device inside of his coat. He then sat up on the car and swung his legs over the edge of it, jumping down to his cowboy booted feet.

"You got dat file for me, bruvh?"

"The money first," He snapped his fingers and coiled his hand like *fork it over.*

The hit-man's eyes zeroed in on the manila envelope peeking outside of Sebastian's jacket.

"It's in the car."

The man rolled his eyes and blew hot air, puffing out his cheeks in frustration.

"Why don't chu take a walk and get it?" he threw a hand towards his Mercedes. "I've got otha people I needa see, ya know, buddy?"

The assassin threw up his hands in surrender and said, "Alright, alright, alright, hold ya horses." He retreated to the vehicle, unlocking it with a black oval shaped remote as he approached. The doors clicked unlocked and he pulled the back door ajar. Tucking his keys inside of his coat with one hand, he leaned inside with the other. When he came back out his hand was inside of a wrinkled brown paper bag. He closed the door shut and took three steps.

"Is that for me?" Sebastian smiled, eying the bag.

"Yep," Julian lifted the bag and...*Blam! Blam! Blam! Blam!*

The front of the brown paper bag shredded as flames flickered through the bottom of it, ruining the bag and tatting up Sebastian's chest. Once the bullets were through with him, his chest looked like it had been hit with a flurry of rotten tomatoes. His eyes widen with a surprise of a lifetime and he gasped for air. He staggered backwards and dropped the manila envelope, falling to the ground. Coolly, calmly and casually, Julian whistled Dixie as he strolled on over, pulling the tattered brown paper bag from off of his Desert Eagle. Smoke wafted from its barrel and evaporated in the night's air. Standing over his kill, he continued his whistling and tilted his head to the side as he studied the shocked expression he wore before he met with death. Right after, he kneeled down and picked up the manila envelope which was speckled with blood. Rising to his feet and with his gun still in his hand, he pulled out the documents and looked them over. A wicked smile inherited his face when he realized that he had the information that he was looking for.

****

Anton flipped the tinted black visor of his helmet down and mounted his bike. Next, he punched in his destination on the built in high tech navigational system. The screen glowed and an image of the world appeared. The globe rotated around and around and then a description of where the destination was located emerged on the display. A green dot with an arrow above it glowed on and off making beeping sounds. Taking a quick glance down below him at the screen, he leaned forward, wrapping his leather gloved hands around the handlebars and positioning his booted feet. He revved up the engine and took off. Once he punched a button on the kilt of his right handlebar, up ahead the wall of the bunker opened and lead down a paved path that would eventually connect to a city street.

Anton activated the headset inside of his helmet and began a conversation.

"Heyyyyy, pretty lady." He spoke happily.

"Hey, baby boy." A feminine voice responded.

"What chu up to?"

"I'm headed to this meeting right now."

"Oh yeah? Who are you gonna go see?"

"Frost."

"Frost?"

"Yep."

Vroooooom!

The motorcycle flew up the path, leaving debris in the night's chilled air. Anton glanced up at the sky and saw the beautiful moon. It glowed. Its image shone on the tinted glass of his visor. He eyed it for a time before focusing on the road ahead and allowing his mind to drift off to another time. It was the time that he had made a connection that would be essential in gaining him his new found wealth.

Flashback

Anton had just driven into the garage of his house and dismounted his motorcycle when he heard hurried footsteps coming up behind him. He went to turn around and was clocked over the head by a dark mysterious man. As soon as he hit the floor the man restrained his wrists and ankles. Next, he tossed him over his shoulder and carried him off. He dumped him inside of the trunk and pulled off.

Sometime later Anton awoke tied to a chair and sitting at a table. He sat up with his head hung and the top of his scalp visible. His chest rose and fell with every breath that he took. The basement he was sitting inside of was dark save for the light illuminating from the yellowish light bulb dangling above his head. In the shadows there were three people. Two of them were men and one of them was a woman. They were visible from the waist down.

"Anton Jackson." A voice said from the darkness like he was a real piece of work and took a deep breath.

"Who the fuck are you?" Anton glared up at him.

A tall white man emerged from the shadows away from his associates. He was a hefty fella with a nest of brownish red hair and a thick comb mustache that over lapped his top lip. His eyes were grey but looked dull blue. His seriousness was etched across his face. He was in a plaid shirt and a blue jacket. His firearm was concealed in a worn black leather holster on his hip.

"Special Agent Casey McCready," he flashed him his badge before concealing in the recess of his jacket where he'd gotten it. Afterwards, he picked up a chair and planted it before his detainee. Adjusting his holster on his waistline, he cleared his throat with a fist to his mouth and sat down. He locked eyes with Anton and steepled his meaty hands.

"Should I be star struck, Special Agent Casey McCready?" he stated with a smirk that curled the end of his lips.

"Humph...I must say, Mr. Jackson, I am thoroughly impressed with your work," he looked over his shoulders, snapping his fingers and motioning someone over with his hand. "Steel, let me get that file." Anton's eyes looked to where McCready was talking and a black lady with short *dreads and rich chocolate skin emerged. She was dressed in a white blouse, cream blazer and blue jeans. Her demeanor screamed don't fuck with me and so did the expression on her face. She seemed to be the storm to Agent McCready's calm.*

Agent Steel handed McCready a file and he thanked her. Once he placed the file on the table-top, he opened it and started sitting pictures down in front of his capture so that he could see them. In each of the pictures there was a man or woman that had been brutally murdered. If the average person were to have seen these grisly images they would have vomited.

"Dammmn, somebody fucked them niggaz up." *Anton studied the photos with raised eyebrows looking to be amazed at how some of the victims had been done. He looked up at McCready and said, "Y'all catch up with homie yet? I mean, with all of these niggaz he laid out I know for sure that he's looking at the death penalty."*

"Cut the shit," Steel slammed her fist down on the table and mad dogged Anton. "We know it was you."

"Really, bitch? Well, prove it." Anton clenched his jaws and veins pulsated at his temples. His nostrils flared and he breathed heavily from them.

"I thought you'd never ask." a third voice spoke from the shadows and Special Agent Tanner stepped out with three Ziploc bags which he placed on the table-top before the suspect, one by one. Inside of the first bag there was a hair, in the second there was gauze with blood on it, and inside of the third there was a piece of chewed gum. "From that last job you did, we've got your hair, your blood and the gum you'd chewed. You really fucked yourself with this one." the slender dark haired agent held up the Ziploc containing the chewed gum up and then

44

tossed it back down on the table-top. He then smiled triumphantly. Inside of his head he was thinking that he and his colleagues had the young nigga by the balls.

"Clever. Reallllly fucking clever," Anton laughed causing the agents to exchange glances. "But all of the jobs I did were, and still, are untraceable to me. I am a professional, an expert if you will. So I could never, ever, move so sloppily."

"Ah ha," McCready held up a plump finger and smiled, showcasing his coffee stained teeth. "Maybe you're professional now, but what about way back then."

Anton balled up his face and twisted his lips. He gave McCready the side eye and angled his head. "Way back when?"

Hearing that, McCready picked up a remote control from off of the table-top that Anton hadn't notice the entire time that he had been sitting at the table. The hefty agent turned to his left and pointed the remote at a "32 box television set sitting on a black iron push cart. As soon as the screen came on, the volume went from three to a hundred so that everyone could hear it.

Anton was genuinely surprised about what he saw on the TV's screen before him. No one could have guessed this though. The young hitter had a face chiseled out of stone and eyes that didn't tell a damn thing of what he was thinking inside of his head. He was taught this by his mentor; never let them see you sweat, and he never did.

The agents looked back and forth between the television and Anton with shit eating grins on their faces figuring that they had him right where they wanted him. Playing on the screen was the very first murder that the young gunner had ever committed. Five years ago Anton was beaten badly by a drug dealer named Kilo for stealing his truck and taking it to a chop shop for a profit. Eureka caught up with the nigga and carved his ass up like a Thanksgiving turkey. Later, he abducted her and strung her up in a closed down supermarket's freezer. It was there that he whipped her naked back with a homemade whip for several days, and eventually left her there to die.

Eureka managed to free herself from her bondages and fled home. When Anton found out what had happened he took it upon himself to exact revenge. He concocted a plan with a local crackhead by the name Fred to murder Kilo. The junky's job was to distract czar long enough for Anton to creep up on him and leave his fucking thoughts on the dashboard. The first shot caught Kilo by surprise but didn't kill him. He went for his gun and Fred tried to stop him. They scuffled just long enough for Anton to finish the job, and that was sending the czar to meet his maker. With the deed done, the homicide suspects fled to an alley several blocks away. It was there in that alley that Anton discovered that Fred had been scratched up in his scuffle with Kilo. He knew that once the police caught up with the fiend that he'd eventually tell his part in the murder and he'd never see sunlight again. With that in mind, the young nigga murked him out and got the fuck out of dodge.

Anton's murdering of Crackhead Fred in the alley was being shown on the television screen. The last scene was of him tucking his gun and throwing a hood over his head, before looking both ways and fleeing down the street.

McCready turned off the TV with the remote control and turned back around to Anton. He and his associates had victorious smiles plastered on their faces. Unbeknownst to Anton he had been filmed that night by some pill head with a camera he'd gotten for his birthday. The kid had unwittingly sold the camera to McCready's teenage son

46

who was taking up video production class in high school. The agent had walked in on his son watching the footage that the pill head had forgotten to erase. He was surprised when he saw that it was Anton that had murdered the crackhead inside of the alley. He felt that he could use this as leverage to try to get the young nigga to do what he wanted.

"Fred and Kilo's murders are enough to have you sent away for the rest of your days, my friend. You'll never see..."

"Save me the speech, homeboy, 'cause I ain't snitching on not one single mothafucking soul." Anton told him like it was, glaring at him. "I played the game and loss. I'll accept my fate like a man. I was born with a cock and balls, notta twat and a pair of tits." he hawked up phlegm and spat it on the photos of the dead persons. "Slap on them cuffs and run me in. I'm tryna get this shit over with."

McCready folded his arms across his chest and took a deep breath. "What if I told you that you can avoid any repercussions for your actions here? What if I told you that I will dispose of this DVD right here and right now, and you can walk right out that door?" he pointed upward towards the basement door.

"I already told you I'm not snitching. Now, if you come at me like that again, I'm gonna take it as a sign of disrespect, and you and I are gonna have ourselves a situation."

"You've got quite the mouth on you, boy." Steel glared at him and twisted her lips.

"I've got quite the dick on me too, gorgeous." he smiled, winked and blew her a kiss.

"We've gotta proposition for you, junior, and it doesn't involve you telling on anyone." Tanner sat on the *edge of the table and folded his hands in the lap of his tight ass jeans, showcasing the handle of the gun in his holster.*

"I'm listening." Anton gave him his undivided attention.

"The C.I.A can always use someone with your exceptional skills on our team." he informed him. *"You come to work for us putting heads to bed and you'll earn diplomacy, and more money than you can count, how about that?"*

"Sounds great, but I like doing my own thing."

"Oh, you can still do your own thing on the side, but you'll be working primarily with us."

The agents watched Anton as he looked to be thinking things over. Once he drew his conclusion, he gave them a nod and they released him from his restraints. He was made to sign some forms that would certify his employment to the Central Intelligence Agency and then given the DVD in which captured him murdering Crackhead Fred. Next, he was driven to their headquarters where he was given a tour and met some very important people. Before he made his departure he was given a cell phone that they would use to contact him whenever they needed him. He was also told that money would be deposited into the account that they set up for him, whether he executed a task for them that month or not.

Present

Pulling his thoughts back to the here and now, Anton mashed the gas pedal and blew past a light just as it turned red. He became nothing more than a flicker of light on those city streets that night.

CHapteR 3

Tristan sat at the bar hunched over a glass of something dark. From the expression on his face and his body language anyone looking could tell that something was wearing on the man. That something was what he'd have to come to grips with or it would forever eat at his soul and leave him dead long before his time. Tristan was a man of a tall stature and athletic physique. His smooth copper complexion was compliments of his Dominican heritage and his crown of short curly hair was tapered off, leading to a goatee that aligned his jaw line perfectly. One look at him would put one in the mind of a basketball player or super model, but that thought couldn't be further away from the truth. The cat was a part time bouncer at the Kitty Kat; a hole in the wall strip joint out in West L.A that every lowlife and two bit criminal visited.

Tristan remembered the night he'd made his bones. A couple of knuckleheads had come in that night stark drunk and looking for trouble. They'd tried to convince one of the girls to come back to their house with them but she wasn't having it. So they got it in their minds to kidnap her. They would have gotten away with it too, had it not been for Tristan Toretto being on the job.

Flashback

"Helllllp! Somebody help me!"

"Haa! Haa! Haa! Haa! Haa! Haa," Tristan hauled ass down the sidewalk, looking like a blur as he moved through the crowd, gun in hand, knocking mothafuckaz out of the way. "Move!" He shoved a young man aside and he fell up against a group of other people walking in the opposite direction. "Fuck outta my way!" he bowled down the center of a pack dudes heading toward the strip club.

"Damn, nigga, you stepped on my fuckin' shoes!"

"Fuck dem shoes!" Tristan hollered out, barely turning his head over his shoulder. At his waist he had his banger gripped. He'd just rounded the corner where the three niggaz had disappeared with one of the exotic dancers from the strip club. He slowed his roll as he bent the corner, slowly lifting that steel, ready to pop off. His eyes widen and he gasped. On high alert, his head snapped from left to right, wondering where the fuck they had gone. It was like they had evaporated into thin air.

Screeeeech!

The sound of squealing tires drew his attention to the center of the block where he found a silver "96 Chevy Impala, busting a U-turn in the middle of the street. He took off after them, running as fast as he could, head up and fists balled. He breathed huskily, chest leaping up and down as he moved forward. His legs looking like blurs. By this time his face was shiny from sweat and perspiration was running down the back of his neck. His eyes stayed on the back of the Impala. He was catching up with it being that it had to stop at an upcoming intersection. He caught halfway up with the vehicle when the stop light turned green and the car kept going.

"Shit!" he fumed, feeling like he was missing his chance. He darted out into the middle off the intersection and got blinded by headlights coming from his right. Turning his head toward it, he narrowed his eyelids and threw up his hand. His eyes went wild and he dropped his jaw. Boom! He went over the hood and dropped his gun, hitting the surface on his side wincing. Pain racked his body as he rolled back and forth, holding himself. Hearing the kidnapped girl screaming for help inside of his head recharged the battery in his back. After fighting back the

pain he was feeling, he peeled his eyelids open and got upon his hands, scanning the ground for his burner. Seeing it ahead, he scrambled over to it and snatched it up.

"Hey, man, are you alright?" The driver of the car that had hit him asked as he held open the driver side door of his vehicle. With that, Tristan whipped around. He gripped his weapon with both hands and pointed it at him. The sight of the banger made the driver's eyelids and mouth shoot open.

"I'ma need to confiscate your vehicle, homeboy." he slowly approached him, cars whipping back and forth across their paths.

"Sure, bro, she's yours."

"Thanks." Tristan hopped behind the wheel and sat his piece on the front passenger seat, slamming the door shut behind him. Switching gears, he floored it away from the scene, boot mashing the pedal. He narrowed his eyelids and leaned forward, seeing the brake lights of the Impala up ahead. "I got you." he frowned, face displaying concentration and determination. "I got you dick-heads now." he mashed the pedal to the floor and the engine revved up, boosting the car's speed. The windows of the whip were open so he could feel the night's air on his face, as well as its ruffling of his black T-shirt. The cars parked on either side of him looked like colorful blurs to him as he blew past them, going one hundred miles an hour in a twenty-five miles an hour zone. The Impala was coming up quickly. He could see two silhouettes through the back tinted window, moving around like they were fighting. Something told him that it was Star putting up one hell of a fight, trying to not be violated, or even worse, murdered. "I'm on my way, Star, hang in there, lil' momma, just hang on!" he grabbed his head bussa from the front passenger

seat and tucked it in between the driver seat and the console. Gripping the steering wheel with both hands, he tilted his head down and glared up at the back of the Impala. Clenching his jaws, he mashed the pedal even further, causing the hand of the speedometer to spin around to the other side hastily. The engine's build up was furious, growling like an angry lioness defending its young. "Here we go, baby girl, here we go! Sit tight!" Boom! He rammed the back of the Impala, causing him to jerk in his seat and ruin the opposite car's bumper, causing it to fishtail. Seeing the driver trying to regain control of his ride, Tristan rammed that son of a bitch again. Boom! The vehicle's tires screeched and it spun around twice before crashing its rear into a light post on a residential street, bending it in half. For a time there was silence, save for the moaning and groaning of the whip's passengers from the violent accident. All of them wore either forming knots on their foreheads or bleeding gashes, moving about lazily as they were barely conscious.

"Uhhhhhh."

The driver of the wrecked vehicle peeled his bloody face up from the steering wheel, head bobbling about. He looked up through the windshield to see a Jeep Cherokee coming to a hasty stop. The driver side door of the SUV came open and its driver stepped out. His heart punched at his chest bone seeing that he had a gun in his hand and was hurriedly moving in his direction, checking the magazine of his weapon. He looked pissed off, really pissed off.

"Holy shit!" the man came around feeling as though his life was in danger. He struggled to get his heater out of the glove box. For some goddamn reason it wouldn't open. It was locked. That's when he realized that the key was on the same ring as his car keys. He went to pull the keys out of

the ignition and that's when his door was snatched open. A very heated Tristan snatched his punk ass out of the seat and slammed him up against the side of the car, smacking him upside the head with that tool. Tristan squared his jaws and assaulted him viciously, staining his gun crimson and swelling up his entire face. When he drew back to hit him again, he froze, cheeks swelling and deflating as he stared at him.

Tristan noticed that his victim's head was hanging at a funny angle and he was breathing awkwardly. Seeing that he'd whipped him out, he let him fall to the ground. That's when he heard the front passenger door creaking open. The passenger was about to point his gun and fire but before he could, Tristan stuck his heater through the driver side window and shot him in the crotch. He howled in pain and fell to the surface holding what was left of himself. Afterwards, the hero moved to the back door of the car and snatched it open. In the backseat he found a buff, bald head nigga with his eyes rolled to their whites. He was out of it, moaning; a lump on his forehead.

Tristan grabbed the nigga by the front of his shirt and pulled him out, letting his big ass hit the asphalt. He knew homeboy was fucked up but he didn't give a shit. For good measure, he kicked him in the stomach and knocked the wind out of him. He hollered and doubled over, holding his torso. Tristan tucked his thang at the small of his back and reached back inside of the ride, taking Star by her manicured hand and helping her out, one clear bottom stiletto at a time. Her face was wet from crying and her eyeliner was running.

"Star, you straight?" he held her at arm's length, staring into her eyes. She was crying frantically and trembling all over like she was naked in 30 below weather.

Star brought her quivering fingers up before her eyes and made an ugly face, mouth shivering. She broke down sobbing uncontrollably, throwing herself into her savior and wrapping her arms around his neck. "You're gonna be alright, sis. Just let it go, let it all out." she squeezed him tighter and he swept his hand up and down her back, trying his best to sooth her. The experience was very traumatic and had her shaken up. A time later she quieted down and peeled herself away from him. Right then police cruiser sirens filled the air. She wiped her dripping eyes with a curled finger and thanked him. He acted like it was nothing, but truthfully he was doing some action movie type of shit out there that night. Star had never had anyone go all out for her like he had so she was very grateful. Tristan was always a gentleman with her and the rest of the girls, she appreciated that.

Star's brows furrowed when she saw blood running from the sleeve of the hero's T-shirt. He frowned noticing her looking at him strangely. Following her eyes he spotted what had her attention and waved it off. It was a gunshot wound.

"That ain't about nothing, I'll be alright."

"You sure?" she took hold of his arm and examined closely.

"Yeah, it's just a flesh wound."

Present

Tristan finished the last of his drink and sat the glass down on the bar-top. He then motioned the bartender over with a wave of his hand. The older gentleman threw up a hand for him to give him a second as he was busy mixing a drink for another patron. Once he was done, he dropped a cherry into the glass along with a black straw before sitting it on a napkin, sliding it before the man that had ordered it.

The man thanked him and tossed him down a tip, along with the cost of his alcoholic beverage. The bartender thanked him with a slight nod of his head, stashing his tip in his pocket and putting the rest of the money he was given inside of the register. After pushing the drawer of the register shut, he headed back down the bar in Tristan's direction, wiping his hands on his black apron.

"What can I get for you, Trist?" he asked, placing his wrinkled hands on the bar-top. He was a skinny, dark skinned gent with a graying afro and salt and pepper chin stubble.

"Fill her up, Nigel." he gestured toward the empty glass, head bobbing about. His eyes had taken on a glassy, eerie look and he wore a space out expression across his face. It was safe to say that this nigga was shit faced. That's exactly what Nigel noticed as he stood before him with a wrinkled forehead, angling his head as he observed him.

"Aye, Trist, why don't chu call it a night, man? That liver of yours isn't gon' be worth jack shit by the time you're through with it," he reasoned, picking up the telephone and reaching to press one of the numbered buttons. "I'ma call you a cab, I know you aren't fit to get behind the wh…"

Tristan leaned over the bar and held down the button that hung up the line. He then settled back down on his stool wearing that silly ass expression on his face.

"One more drink. One more drink and you can call me a fuckin' spaceship to mars for all I care."

Nigel thought on it and took a deep breath, hanging up the telephone. "Alright, one more drink and that's it." he pointed his finger into his face, giving him a stern look, looking like a father that was scolding his child.

Tristan threw up his hands in surrender, holding eye contact with him. "Aye, this here is your fine establishment. Whatever you say goes. One more drink and my ass will vamoose." he slurred.

"Okay, then." he went on about the task of fixing him another drink. When he finished, he slid it forth and a couple of wrinkled bills were dropped on the bar-top. The bartender scooped the bills up and put them in the cash register, pushing it back shut.

Tristan pushed up from the bar slowly, legs slightly buckling as his drunken ass tried to stand upright. He picked up the glass and held up a finger.

"Ladies and gentlemen," he slowly spun around the establishment holding up the glass of dark liquor, waves going across its surface from his movements. "I present to you all, my last drink of the night," he pointed his finger to his chest. "It's been real." He went to down his hard liquor and was bumped into. This caused him to spill the alcohol on his shirt and shoes. A ripple of lines went across his forehead and he turned around to the cat that had bumped into him. He found a bear of a man in a feathered black brimmed hat, gold frames and necklace. He'd just sat down on his stool beside a lovely young lady that looked like she could star in a rap music video. The giant seemed to have noticed that he'd bumped into Tristan but he didn't give a flying fuck. A frowning Tristan looked to Nigel who shrugged as he was popping off the top of a Corona for another patron. Tristan then sat his glass down and tapped the big man on his shoulder. Perturbed, he threw up a hand like *Leave me the fuck alone,* so he tapped him on the shoulder again. This time harder to make sure he got the mothafucka'z attention.

56

The man spun around on his stool, the skin on his forehead bunched up as his chubby, gold ring bearing fingers took pulls from the half of cigar that was pinched between them. His lips puckered up and blew out a cloud of smoke into Tristan's face, causing him to narrow his eyelids. With a fist to his mouth, he coughed and fanned the smoke away. That shit choked him and smelled foul as hell.

"Fuck you won't, man? Can't you see I'm busy courting this young tender here?" He referred to the beauty sitting beside him wearing a Bob and a sexy form fitting red dress.

"Yeah, I can see that," Tristan assured him. "Can you see that you bumped into me and made me spill this fourteen dolla glass of liquor on my goddamn shirt?"

The giant looked him up and down with a twisted face, observing him like he wasn't much to look at it. Without saying another word, he reached inside of his leather jacket and pulled out a wad of dead presidents. He removed the gold money-clip and peeled off two fifty dollar bills, throwing it into his face.

"Take it to the cleaners, nigga." he spun back around to the woman he was spitting G at, sticking his mula back inside of his leather jacket. The insult left Tristan as hot as an African summer. He could literally feel his blood boiling and popping with bubbles. He looked around the bar and found every single eye in the joint on him. He had been made to feel like a world class chump. He couldn't allow himself to go out like a bitch ass nigga. Fuck all of that. There wasn't a drop of ho in his blood. Squaring his jaws, Tristan balled his hands into fists causing veins to form all over them.

There was a feral growl and then a kick to the legs of the stool the big man was sitting on. The stool flew out from underneath him and his big ass went slamming to the floor, grimacing. The broad he was talking to shot up from her chair surprised and grabbing her handbag, hastily getting the fuck out of the way.

"Ahhhhh, you broke my ribs," the big man gritted, holding his side and rolling from side to side.

"The bigga they are, the harder they fall," Tristan smiled and picked up the big man's brimmed hat. He placed it on his head and looked at his reflection in the mirror behind the bar, adjusting his new hat. Smiling with satisfaction, he thumped the brim of it and set his sights back on his victim, taking on a menacing expression. "Who's afraid of the big bad wolf? The big bad wolf! The big bad wolf!" he sung before flying off of the handle, kicking him hard as hell in his ribs causing him to unleash a sound that a wounded whale would. From there he went in on him, kicking him, stomping him, and throwing beer bottles and empty glasses at his head from the bar- top. Niggaz tried to get him to stop but he started swinging on them, laying them out too. He didn't give a mad ass fuck though. He was already heated about the shit he was dealing with so this was the perfect opportunity for him to relieve some of his stress. "Mark ass, punk ass nigga! Tryna make me look like a ho out this bitch!" His foot came down and from the side rapidly. He was pounding this nigga the fuck out.

Everybody in the bar stood by observing Tristan put down that work; some of them cringing and others just watching. He heard someone ordering him to stop but he didn't pay them any mind. He was in a zone and taking out his frustrations on homeboy beneath his shoe. Suddenly, he felt himself being grasped by the shoulder and pulled backwards. In a flash, he whipped around and swung his fist. *Bwhrack!* The solid blow surprised the policeman. He staggered back toward his partner holding the bloody lower half of his face. Tristan sobered up real quick seeing that he'd fucked up big time. The policeman's partner drew his gun and ordered him to put his hands behind his head and get down on his knees. Taking a deep breath and wearing a face of defeat, he did as he was ordered. The policeman moved in, holstering his weapon and cuffing him. As soon as the policeman pulled him up to his feet, he smacked the brim from off his head. Right after, the cop he had assault swooped in and punched him in the gut, doubling him over. The blow brought tears to his eyes. The wind had been knocked out of him and it hurt like a son of a bitch.

"The perfect ending to a fucked up night," Tristan winced as he was manhandled out of the bar by the police.

*****

Julian pulled up to the location that was on one of the many photos that he'd stolen from Sebastian. Killing his headlights and executing the engine, he looked back and forth between the picture in his lap and the windshield. His eyes scanned the crowd of Bloods that were shooting the shit and indulging in their poison of choice. He was looking for Fear's cousin who was also from the same Blood set as him, The Eastside Outlaws 20s. He figured it would be through him that he'd uncover the AWOL hit-man's location. In the photo there was a twenty something dark skinned kid of average stature. He was mad dogging and holding up the placard for his mug shot. Julian shuffled through the next couple of photos of him which were of the areas of his body that had tattoos.

The one that was most noticeable to him was the one on the side of his neck, Lil' Fear.

Julian couldn't make out the nigga that he was looking for from where he was parked, so there wasn't any doubt in his mind that he'd have to get up close. This wasn't a big deal. He was expecting this. After sliding the photos and documents back inside of the manila envelopment, he placed them inside of the glove box and closed it shut. Next, he opened the console and removed a small bottle of green fluid and a syringe. Once he stashed these items on his person, he hopped out of the car and casually walked across the street. The closer he drew near the crowd he'd just scoped minutes ago, the louder the music and conversation grew.

"Yo' who dis?" one of the Blood's tapped his homie, seeing the European hit-man approaching. This got the rest of his homies attention and they all turned in his direction.

"Kill that stereo, Baby Mann." Another Blood gave the order. A shorter gangbanger ducked off to his Cutlass Supreme and murdered Future's *God Bless The Trap Nigga's*. He then hopped back out of the whip and posted back up with his niggaz.

As soon as Julian stepped upon the curb, he found the gangbangers encircling him like a ring of fire. When this happened homeboy didn't even break a sweat, he'd been in the face of danger countless times before.

"Good evening gentlemen, I'm looking for a chap by the name of Jayshawn Simpson. I believe you chaps refer to him as Lil' Fear, or Lil' Fearless." Julian looked around at all of the hard faces of the men before him. The one to his right took a pull from his thinly rolled blunt and blew a cloud of smoke into his face, causing him to narrow his eyelids.

"You hear this nigga accent? Fuck this fool from?" Baby Mann questioned his homies.

"I don't know," another Blood's face twisted, shaking his head confusingly. "England or some shit."

"Man, I don't give a fuck where dis nigga from," old boy barked on his niggaz. This was the same dude that had blown the smoke into Julian's face. "Check it, we don't know no Fear, homeboy," he flicked what was left of his blunt away, sending embers flying. "But I'll tell you what I do know, I know you got about five seconds to beat the street 'fore we smash on yo' mothafucking ass!"

Lil' Fear, Julian made the ink of the young man's neck that was popping off at the mouth.

At that moment, the hit-man felt one of the bloods step behind him. His eyes shot to their corners and then he heard the hammer of a pistol being cocked. This time a voice was shouting a warning to him, *danger, danger, danger!* His eyes quickly came back around to the Blood before him. Feeling the hostile stares of all of the gangbangers in his presence caused the corner of his lip to curl up.

These niggaz don't know what they're in for, he thought to himself.

"Humph." he said, already knowing that he was going to make short work of his opposition.

"I suggest you get the fuck up from outta here, homie, 'fore the coroners are scraping yo' thoughts off this curb." the nigga that had blown the smoke spoke again, clenching his jaws so tight that they pulsated. Julian didn't say a word, he just stood there mad dogging the man and clenching his fists so tight that the veins in them bulged. "Are you deaf, Blood? I said beat it!"

"Fuck you!" the assassin spat with emphasis, fists trembling they were clenched so firmly. The groves of his forehead deepened and his eyes darkened. He brought his chin to his chest and glared up at the asshole in front of him. He'd planned on killing every last one of them, but this mothafucka Lil' Fear was going to suffer the worse. That was until he bled him for all of the information that he needed.

With the gauntlet having been laid down, the Blood gave the cat behind Julian a nod. When this signal was given he lifted a silver .357 revolver, the street lights reflected off it and caused it to gleam. As soon as he brought pressure to the trigger, the killer's ear slightly jumped and his eyes shot to their corners again. He listened closely, hearing the sound of metal as the trigger was pulled back. Then there was the pin slamming into the butt of the bullet and the chamber clicking as it turned counter clockwise. There was a loud clasp that resonated, sounding like two aluminum trays banging together. Fire spat from the barrel of the shiny pistol and when it did, Julian snapped his head to the left. Everything seemed to be moving in slow motion at this time. The bullet whizzed right past the hit-man's ear, ruffling the collar of his coat. The man that attempted to blast on him eyes bulged and his jaw dropped. He couldn't believe what he had just witnessed and neither could the rest of his homies.

"Arrghhhhh," The nigga standing before him threw his head back and hollered, putting his uvula and every cavity inside of his mouth on display. The bullet that had exited the revolver burst through his shoulder and went through the back of him. He went reeling backwards and crashing to the black spotted, cracked sidewalk.

Julian grabbed the wrist of the nigga that had shot the revolver. He twisted it to the right causing him to drop it when the pain jolted through it. Once the gunman shrilled, he used his arm to flip him over his shoulder and slam him on his back. Quickly, he picked up his .357 and shot him dead in his mouth, his bloody brain fragments splattering beneath his head. With his expiration, Julian whipped around to a Blood that was coming off of his waistline with a .9mm. Before the weapon could clear his Dickies, he was getting three to the chest. Agony was written across his face as he fell to his knees with a smoking chest, dropping his gun. Hearing hurried footsteps at his back; Julian picked up his gun and spun around, lifting both of his weapons. He aimed at the remaining Blood as he sprinted up the street, trying to clear the block with his life. The assassin walked forward slowly, weapons dancing in his hands as he shot them off. He heard the grunts of excruciation as the hot slugs pierced his victim's back. The nigga collapsed face first, his arms and legs flailing in the air.

Having laid down the last gangbanger, the night had grown as silent as the grave save for the approaching police cruisers sirens that seemed to be coming somewhere far off in the distance. Julian cleaned off the burners with the lower half of his shirt and let them fall to the surface. Afterwards, he turned around to homeboy that had gotten shot through the shoulder, pulling a pair of latex gloves from out of his coat's pocket and pulling them on. Watching him hold his shoulder and scramble upon his feet, he pulled out a syringe and a small bottle of a lime green sedative. He slid the needle through the top of the bottle and drew its contents into the syringe needle. Next, he stuck the bottle back inside of his coat and squirted a little of the liquid out of the needle. Speed walking towards the sole survivor, all he could hear were his own dress shoes clicking on the ground and his victim's pained breathing. The gritting gangbanger had just looked over his shoulder when he grabbed him underneath his chin and pulled his head back, turning it to the side. His eyes found a plump vein bulging out the side of his neck and that's where he let the needle pierced him, injecting the sedative. The gangbanger's eyes rolled to their whites and he moaned right before passing out cold. Discarding the syringe, Julian zip cuffed his wrists and ankles. He then hoisted him over his shoulder and carried him off to his car, whistling Dixie. Once he opened the trunk, he dumped his ass in there and slammed it shut, walking over to the driver's side. He opened the door and slid in behind the wheel, resurrecting the engine and pulling off. As he drove along listening to Classical music, he began to formulate all kinds of wicked torture methods he could use to get the nigga in his trunk to tell him what he wanted to know about Fear.

****

Eureka stood outside of Newton Division precinct adjusting her beanie on her head and lifting her collar of her coat to combat the wind. After lifting her sleeve to check the time on her watch, she stashed her hands inside of her coat and tapped her foot impatiently. She'd posted bail for Tristan a little over three hours ago at 3D Bail Bonds and had been waiting for him to be released ever since. She wasn't the slightest bit surprised when she'd gotten the call that night especially after what had happened between them.

Flashback

Eureka quivered feeling his tongue trace her chocolate nipples and suck on her areolas like a starving baby. She gasped and pulled at the sheets, licking her lips. He mashed her breasts together and jumped back and forth between them, giving them their equal amounts in attention. A length of saliva trailed from his bottom lip to her left breast when he pulled back from it, wiping his mouth with the back of his fist. He placed both hands on the sides of her torso, sensually kissing her down her flat stomach and pass her navel. He gently separated her thick, juicy legs and revealed her beautifully shaved pussy. He traced it with the tip of his tongue and then slid it up and down the opening of her V, causing her to squirm and turn her head every which way. She pulled the sheets tight into her palms, leaving some of the fabric peeking out between her fingers. When she attempted to shut her legs he forced them back open like, You gone give me this pussy tonight. Starting at the bottom of the opening of her treasure, he slid his tongue upwards very slowly until he met her swollen clit. Quickly, he flicked his tongue back and forth across that small flap of meat. This made her holler out and try to shut her legs again, but he forced them back open. He fingered her spot and steadily flicked his tongue across her clit. Feeling his hot breath and the moisture of his mouth caused her coochie to get wetter than it was before.

"Mmmmmhmmmm," he made noises as he pleasured her, occasionally glancing up at her to see the different sex faces that she was making. He was pleased to see that he was pleasing her. The sight caused his dick to grow to its full potential. His swollen head was throbbing and oozing pre-cum. He focused on sucking on her love trigger and removed his fingers from out of her middle. They were glistening down to his knuckles. He brought them to her mouth and she sucked on them while she groped her own titties, nipples standing at attention.

Having enough of that, he stood up on his knees and moved in closer between her parted legs. Holding his thick penis at the base, he rubbed his dick head up and down her slit. Right after, he was smacking her pearl with it driving her fucking crazy.

"You won't this dick, baby?" he asked in a sexy, masculine tone. *She grasped both sides of her pillow and pushed her head back into it, halfway burying it. She was moaning and hissing, feeling her pussy oozing her hot liquid.* *"Huh? You hear this dick talking to you?"* he bit down on his bottom lip and smacked his hardened meat against her jewel harder. *Her pussy squirted a little and she winced with pleasure, biting down on her inner jaw.* *"You hear it, baby? Huh? You hear this big mothafucka?"*

"Yesssss!" she rasped.

"What chu want me to do with this mothafucka?" he smacked his dick up against her even harder, wrist working back and forth.

"Fuck me with it." she told him.

"Huh?" he leaned closer and lifted his eyebrows, acting as if he didn't hear her.

"Fuck me with it, papi."

With the command giving, he positioned himself so that he'd be hovering above her. Licking his lips, he pushed himself inside of her. It took a little more pressure for his head to pierce open her walls, but once he parted her he found that her grip was tighter than a pair of baby hands.

"Ooooooh, sssshit," he shut his eyelids and his head shuddered, feeling how good the inside of her was. *Her pussy was heaven on earth and he wanted be her God. Mashing his fists on each side of the bed of her, he drove himself inside of her tunnel. He hit her with half of him, slow stroking her center at first, but then again speeding up, working her faster and faster. At first she was moaning, but then she went to hollering out in pure ecstasy, feeling him pushing in and out of her.*

"Uh! Uh! Uh! Uh!" *She arched her back and wrapped her legs around his waist, his muscular back*

contracted and lifted with each of his thrust, causing his slightly hairy ass to flex. The headboard banged up against the wall fast and hard, but no one else inside of the mansion could hear them because the walls were reasonably thick.

"Ahhhhh!" He threw his head back and his eyelids flickered, as he clenched his jaws. This showcased the bone structure in his face. The veins at his temples, neck and sculpted arms bulged, the more energy he exerted making love to her. He looked down at her face watching her face morphs to different expressions as he dug her out, grinding deep, down inside of that thang. Feeling his member tingling he knew that he was about to cum hard as a mothafucka. "Sssssshit, Reka, I'ma 'bouta bust, babe. Goddamn, here I cum, ma, here I cum!"

"Cum, baby," she rasped, "cum deep up in this pussy." she matched his rhythm, throwing her hips in a circular motion. Both of them were shiny from sweat and ready to cum. She met with her climax first and started shaking but he was quickly coming up behind her. "Fuck me...Oh my God, fuck the shit out of me...."

She called out another man's name and dude sexing her suddenly stopped. All of his semen went soaring back down inside of his nut sack. He stared down at her face with hurt and devastation in his eyes, forehead dripping sweat. She peeled her eyelids open and looked up at him with sorrowful eyes. Her expression read as sorry. Tristan's face transformed into one of hatred and his eyes became glassy. Squaring his jaws, he hauled off and slapped a flame out of her ass. Next, he was hopping up out of the bed and sliding on his sweat pants angrily. He put on his socks and began sliding on his Jordans.

Eureka scrambling out of bed holding her stinging cheek and slipping her panties back on. She had on a wife beater and pajama pants when she saw her man slipping on his hoodie and pulling it over his head.

"Wait!" she reached out to him with one hand while holding the side of her face with the other. He stopped cold in his tracks, slightly turning his head over his shoulder to hear what the fuck she had to say. Although he hated himself for having put his hands on her, he felt that she deserved every inch of his palm that struck her face. He couldn't front about being surprised that she hadn't attacked him for the assault. This was because he knew how she was built and what she did for a living.

"I'm sorry, bae, I really am." Eureka told him.

Hearing this, he slowly turned around to face her, the pain still evident in her eyes.

"Keep that shit a stack, Reka." she nodded yes. "You still love this nigga?"

She stood there for a time, debating on whether or not she should tell him the heart aching truth. She shut her eyelids and swallowed the ball of nervousness that had formed in her throat. When she peeled her eyelids back open, tears came shooting down her cheeks. Staring him dead in his eyes, she hesitantly nodded yes. Tristan dropped his head, his shoulders rising and falling as he took hard, quick breaths. That one hurt him. Shit damn near made his knees buckle. He lifted his head back up and she saw the twinkling in his eyes. It fucked him up knowing that the woman that he was in love with was in love with someone else. Licking his lips, he swallowed his hurt and turned back around. He pulled the door open and slammed it shut, causing the portraits hanging up to rattle. After that Eureka dropped down to her hands and knees. She sobbed loud and hard, dripping tears and snot. Calming down, she slowly got to her feet and approached her dresser. She grabbed her pack of Newport 100s and pulled out a lone cigarette. Right after, she was picking up a Zippo lighter. The metal of the lighter clinked once he snapped the lid open. She cupped her hand around her square and held the golden orange flame at the end of the cancer stick, roasting it. Smoke rose and she fanned it away hastily, narrowing her eyelids. She plopped down on the edge of the bed, taking pulls from the beginning of her cigarette. Her face showing that she had been crying and was now in deep thought.

"Lord," she began, a fresh set of tears flooded down her cheeks. After blowing out smoke from her nose and mouth, she looked up at the ceiling to address God. "It's has been long enough...so, please tell me why is it that I can't get this man outta my system? Huh? I wanna move on with Tristan and give Kingston the family that Anton and I once had." she mashed her Joe out in the ashtray on the dresser and put her hands together in prayer, still focused on the ceiling. "I beg of you father," she dropped down to her knees, "Please, oh please, cleanse me of the man that the streets call Fear.

Present

Eureka blew hard having grown tired of waiting for Tristan to come out of the precinct. She glanced at her watch one more time before thinking fuck it and jogging back up the concrete steps. When she was coming upon the beginning of the stairs the glass doors of the police station was swinging open. Tristan stepped out looking sick and tired. This was because he had a headache from all of the alcohol that he consumed as well as a broken heart. His eyes lingered on Eureka for a time before he went on to thank her for bailing him out. She told him don't mention it and motioned for him to follow her as she hustled down the steps. Once they reached the landing, they started off for

Eureka's vehicle with their hands stashed inside of their pockets. She was moving up ahead but he was right behind her.

"Where's yo' ride at?" Tristan asked, flipping the collar of his jacket up and tucking his chin to his chest. It was colder than a bitch outside and he was trying to keep warm as best as he could.

"I parked around the corner and down the street. Come on," she motioned for him to follow her. Tristan hurried up and jogged over to his lady, coming to a stop beside her. They bent the corner and moved down the sidewalk.

"Where's King?" He looked back and forth between her and the sidewalk as he moved forth.

"He's at home with Alice. He should be asleep by now. It's past his bedtime." She said, pulling up her sleeve and glancing at her watch.

"Good. When we get home we needa talk," He told her. The rest of the ride home he was going to use to collect his thoughts.

Eureka took a deep breath and said, "I know."

She and Tristan hopped in the car and pulled away from the scene.

CHAptER 4

Anton drove into the underground complex and killed his motorcycle, the globe disappeared. Right after, he was dismounting the bike and pulling off his helmet, hanging it on the handlebar. He made his way towards the elevator lobby, shoulders swaying from left to right. En route, he punched the button that activated his Blu-Tooth.

"You still there?" he asked, punching the UP button on the panel, standing before the double doors of the elevator.

"Yes, I'm still here. I take it you've made it."

"Yep, I'm on my way up now."

"You think you shoulda brought Reka along? I mean, you don't know these people too well. For all you know you could be walking into an ambush or something."

"I told you Reka held her guns up a long time ago. Besides, these niggaz ain't that stupid," he studied the map of the building on the wall, taking precautions. In case she was right he needed to know all the escape routes. He believed that it was better safe than sorry. "mothafuckaz know my get down and how I'm built. Let's not forget the people I got backing me, ya feel me?"

"Hahahaha, you're one arrogant prick, you know that?"

"Not arrogant, confident," he stepped inside of the elevator and punched the button of the floor of his destination. He turned around to face the doors just as they were shutting on him. Looking up and spotting the surveillance camera spying in on him. He stepped out of the sight of it and adjusted the .32 handguns concealed in the sleeves of his jacket. Kneeling down, he lifted the leg of his jeans to make sure his knife was still in place. He stood upright just as the double doors parted for him and he stepped out into a long corridor. It had white walls and a black shiny marble floor that he could see his reflection in. At the end of the hall he made two men in expensive suits standing on either side of a door, hands folded at their waists. They saw him at the same time that he acknowledged them. He saw one of them hold his ear bud down in place, lips moving as he informed someone of something. Anton figured he was letting his boss know that he had arrived on schedule. Thinking this, he glanced at his watch and kept forward. He was right on time.

Anton was about three feet away from the door when the guards stepped before him, stopping him from gaining access to the domain. The young killer looked between the men amusingly.

"Turn around and place your hands on the wall!" the guard with the slicked back hair ordered. He and his partner made to pat their visitor down, but he threw up his hands in surrender, hanging his head and shaking it. He looked back up and found the men with bewildered expressions plastered across their faces.

"I'ma keep it a thousand witchu niggaz, I'm packing." he spoke honestly. This caused them to raise their eyebrows and exchange glances. "I gotta .32 stashed in each of my sleeves and a seven inch knife sheathed against my leg. Now, before you think about taking my toys away from me, think again. 'Cause should you test my G, we gon' for damn sure make the five o'clock news out this bitch."

The guard looked like he was weighing it when his buddy tapped him on the shoulder. With this gesture, he leaned forward and listened to what he had to say briefly. The listener nodded his head and pressed his finger down

THE DEVIL WEARS TIMBS IV

on his ear bud, speaking and then again listening to what he was being told.

"Alright, Mr. Frost, I'm sending him right in now."

The guards parted, allowing a clear path to the double doors.

"Excellent choice gentlemen," Anton patted them on the shoulders as he moved past them. They looked at his hands as if they were covered in horse manure. "You saved me some bullets and your families the funeral arrangements. Now, if you'll excuse me, I've gotta go see a man about a dog." As soon as Anton crossed the threshold into the office he noticed that it was dimly lit, except for the moon light shining in through the ceiling to floor window which gave a beautiful view of downtown Los Angeles. Standing before it was Kelvin Frost holding his right hand about the wrist at the lower half of his back. His tailored suit stretched across his broad back and was tight at his biceps. This was because he flaunted a body of pure muscle and had a head so bald and shiny that you could see your reflection in it. On one hand he wore a chunky gold, diamond pinky ring and a Presidential watch. Across his right cheek there was a nasty scar that he'd earned in prison. It was ugly and only added to his menacing appearance. The moon's lighting shone on the front of him, leaving the back of him in darkness.

Anton stood where he was watching him stare out of the window like a man staring out of the window of his beach house, watching the water crash into the shore. The young assassin went to speak, but Frost beat him to the punch.

"Shadow, I'm so glad that you could make it on such short notice." he began without turning his attention away from the window. "Please, have a seat."

As soon as Anton sat down at the desk he noticed the portrait hanging on the wall behind it. It was of Frost and a young girl with braces. She was smiling from ear to ear. The pretty young lady's hair was pulled back into a bun with a colorful flower on the side of it. She wore bright red lipstick and a royal blue kimono dress. Her father was wearing a kimono as well. The only difference being his was black and green. From the way she and her father were dressed and the scenery, Anton could tell that they were over in Japan. He'd been there a couple of times on an assignment. The young nigga was so engrossed in the portrait that he didn't hear the footfalls of Frost as he approached. However, he did see his shadow casted on the wall as he advanced in his direction. When he turned in his direction he saw him carrying two small glasses with ice cubes in them and a clear glass container with a rubber plug containing brown liquor. He figured that it was Cognac. More than likely Louie XIII since that's what he'd been drinking for as long as he'd known him.

Frost sat a glass down before his guest and himself. He filled his glass and was about to fill Anton's until he masked the rim of it with his hand, shaking his head no.

"I'm good."

"Right, you don't drink. I forgot," he plugged the glass container and sat it off to the side. Sitting down on his executive chair, he picked up the glass and swirled its contents around before eventually taking a sip. The bath of flames scorched his throat, but its annoyance was worth it seeing that it was helping him in dealing with his grief.

"Sooooo, what is it that's troubling you that you feel that you need my expertise?"

"My daughter."

"Your daughter?" he frowned. "What happened? Some asshole put his hands on her?"

Without saying another word, Frost sat the glass down on the desktop and pulled open the desk drawer. He removed a manila envelope and opened it, pulling out a host of photographs. One by one, he dropped each photo before the young assassin's eyes. The first one was of Frost's daughter who was also in the portrait hanging above his desk. She was naked in what looked like a prison laundry room with a red ring around her neck, symbolizing that she'd been strangled to death. Her eyes were staring off at nothing and her lips were white while her brown skin was pale; blood trickles were all over the floor. The next photos that followed were of her as well. Anton was mortified by what he'd saw. Although he'd murdered and had done some pretty awful things to those who were more than deserving of it. What he was seeing now looked like some primal animal had done it and not a human being. Seeing something splashing on the desktop, he eyes slowly crept up to see big teardrops falling from Frost's eyes and him sniffling. Of all of his years of knowing him he'd always been a man of strength, but seeing his daughter in such a way had broken him down.

"Excuse me," Frost took the time to pull his handkerchief from his breast pocket and dabbed his eyes dry. Afterwards, he cleared his throat with his fist to his mouth. "My daughter is a CO for Chino correctional facility. This is also where the man that ratted on some associates of mine is being held. Initially, I hired a couple of hitters to exterminate this rodent, but unfortunately his father sent some goons of his own to intervene. Needless to say, his killers annihilated mine and that fuckin' insect slipped from between my fingers." he slammed his fist down on the desktop, rattling the framed portrait of his family and the gold letter opener that was in its holder.

"I hear you, but how did your daughter get caught up in this mess?" Anton leaned forward steepling his hands together on the desktop, his forehead crinkling.

"As a favor to me, my baby girl lured him into the shower room where he was to be slaughter by my men but that's when his people turned out. My daughter left before it all went down but later Raymar caught up with her. He and his men beat her and stuck shanks inside of her cunt. I'm sorry. Gimmie a minute," he wiped his eyes with the handkerchief and took a deep breath. He was having trouble relaying this story. His emotions were overwhelming him. "That son of a bitch wasn't charged for what he did to my daughter and his father had some strings pulled so that he'd be transported to another prison, a prison where I have no influence."

"What is it that you want me to do?" Anton questioned.

"Frost coughed and scooted up to the desk, steepling his hands. "I want chu to find this miserable fuckin' bastard and bring him to me. Bring him to me alive if you can, so that I can pick him apart, piece by piece." Anton nodded his head as he massaged his chin, thinking on it. Wanting him to agree to go on the mission, Frost decided to give him an incentive. "You do this for me and you can write your own check."

"You serious?"

"If there's one thing I don't play about its money," he pulled out his checkbook and took an ink pen from out of his suit, clicking the button at the butt of it and springing the bald point forth. "Here," he sat the pen and the checkbook before Anton. "Whatever dollar amount you write on that line is yours. No questioned asked. You bring me that piece of shit and you'll collect your bounty."

Anton snatched up the pen and opened up a page of the checkbook, scribbling the sum he wanted to bring Raymar back alive. Once he was done, he sat back in his chair waiting for him to deny him the obscene amount of money that he'd asked for. He thought for sure that all of those digits would send him running home, but he would be sadly mistaken.

Anton watched as Frost read over the check, smirking because he just knew that he was going to deny him his quote.

"Deal."

Anton's forehead creased when he saw that homeboy was cool with paying the amount that he requested.

"Deal." he stared him dead in the eyes.

"Half up front, right?"

"Yep."

"Cool. I received a picture text from the man I sent to finish this fucking scumbag off. He was murdered before he could finish the job." Frost's face twisted with animosity as he searched through his cell phone for the picture text he'd received. Once he finally found it he handed the cellular over to Anton. When the young hitter saw who's face it was that Frost's killer had capture before he died, he looked like he had saw a dead man rise from out of his grave and walk towards him. After that look crossed his face, his expression morphed to one of hostility.

"Is everything okay?" Frost's forehead wrinkled seeing the expression on Anton's face.

"It's all good." Anton assured him.

"Swipe to the left and you'll see a picture of that cheddar eating mothafucka, Raymar." He directed him with his finger. Anton did as he was told and found the picture of the cat that he was assigned to bring in. He studied his face for a time before sending it to his own cell phone. Next, he passed the cellular back to Frost, who flipped it closed and sat it down on his desktop.

"I'm glad to hear that you'll accept this assignment. I'll have the first half of your money transferred to your bank account overseas," he relayed. "You should get the confirmation tomorrow morning."

"Great." he stood to his feet and they shook hands.

With that business handled, Anton opened the door and waltz out of the office. He made sure to mad dog the bodyguards, looking them up and down like they weren't shit. Adjusting the collar of his leather jacket, he continued on his way down the corridor and boarded the elevator. Stepping inside, he pressed the button that would bring him to the underground parking complex.

"You hear that? That nigga Fear's alive and he's out here."

"Yeah, I heard. I thought he was long gone for as long as you've been searching for him."

"Nah, I knew his ass wasn't going to stay gon' forever." Anton informed her. "It's like he told me, 'people are creatures of habit and we all love a familiar place'. It makes us feel comfortable. You know how niggaz are about being in a comfort zone. That's why you got fools that gotta girl but still wanna fuck on they baby's momma every now and again."

"True dat."

Ding!

The double doors of the elevator parted and the young hitter came strolling out. He made his way across the parking garage floor with his reflection shone on it.

"I'm so happy I could fucking nut in my pants." he smiled with joy. "I'm getta million dollar payday and a chance to punch the fool's clock that laid down my pop's. Finally, my old man can rest in peace." he slammed his fist into his palm and closed his fingers around it, continuing his stride in the direction of his motorcycle. It was just ahead. It leaned to the side with the support of the kickstand. From the angle it was sitting it looked like it was going to be filmed for a scene in a major motion picture.

"I'm so happy for you, baby." he could hear her jumping up and down excitedly and clapping her hands. "I know how long you've been waiting to get this shot.

"Four years, four long mothafucking years." he squared his jaws and clenched his fists so tight that his knuckles bulged in them. After sliding on his gloves, he slipped on his helmet and mounted the motorcycle. He started her up and adjusted the mirrors of his vehicle. Revving the bike up, he turned the handle bars and mashed the pedal. The finely tuned machine roared and took off, flying throughout the parking lot complex.

"Are you nervous?"

"Hell no. Do you know what I've taken my body through in preparing for this day?" he said, shirt ruffling as he sped against the wind. He looked like a blur zipping in and out of lanes and passing the vehicles on the sides of him. "I've been putting my body through intense training and taking on suicide missions."

"I get the intense training, but why would you take on suicide missions?"

"So I could prove to myself that I don't fear a mothafucking thang."

"Well, is there anything that you fear?"

"Notta man nor God." he sped up and shot through a yellow light just as it was turning red. Right after, cars were zipping back and forth across the intersection. He was a hair from getting slammed into by a pickup truck, but he appeared to be unfazed being that he kept right along talking.

"Really? You're not even afraid of God?"

"Nah. Fuck The Almighty."

"Wow!"

"Why the wow?"

"It's just that I'm shocked that…"

"That I don't bow down to a powerful, mystical character like the rest of the human cattle?" he questioned. "Nah, no thank you, I can see, hear and touch all of my enemies. So I can't see myself on some humble shit when it comes to a person that I don't even know exists. That's blind faith. Fuck that, you gotta show me something."

There was silence.

"You still there?"

"I'm sorry but, ummm, you caught me off guard with that last statement."

"I don't know why. You've known me long enough to know how I am."

"True."

"But aye, look, I need time to clear my head so I'ma get up witchu later."

"Alright, baby. I love you."

"Dido." he disconnected the call and kept on his way.

Anton vanished into Los Angeles' traffic and blended in with the back lights and headlights of other vehicles. He could tell what road that Fear and Raymar were on from the picture that he was shown. If he knew Fear then he would get off of the road as soon as possible and lay low in a shitty motel. A place where he thought no one would come looking for him. Now, Anton didn't know exactly which motel he would hole up in, but he was banking on it to be the grand daddy of all fucked up places to duck off in.

CHaptER 5

Tristan stood leaning up against the kitchen counter with his arms folded across his chest. His eyes were focused on the linoleum as Eureka went about the task of making them a couple cups of coffee. When she was finally done she went to pass him his cup, but she could tell that his mind was somewhere else. This was why she had to call him a couple of times to get his attention.

"Huh?" he looked up having been pulled from his thinking. "Oh, thanks." He took the cup of coffee and sipped. His eyes locked with hers as she held her cup with two hands and took a sip.

"Spit it out." She told him and licked her lips.

"'Sup?"

"I know you've got something on your mind, Trist." She leaned against the counter beside him, looking over her cup of Joe as she took another sip.

"Did you ever love me?" he looked her square in the eyes. This question stopped her from indulging any further from her cup.

She looked up at the ceiling and took a deep breath, trying to figure out how to say what was on her mind. Coming to a conclusion, she looked to him with eyes that bled the truth.

"I loved you, but I was never in love witchu." She told him straight up behind moistening eyes. It hurt her to hash the hard truth but she knew that there was no time like the present for him to hear it. For a while they held one another's gaze. Tristan's expression was plain and he was thankful that only he could hear his heartbreak. Truthfully, he couldn't be mad at her. She told him all about Fear in the beginning and let him know that he was taking a gamble in dealing with her. She let it be known that if there was ever a possibility that she and him could reunite that she would take it. Figuring that she would never truly give herself to someone that had murdered her father, Tristan decided to take a risk at a game of chance. He wanted to be with her so badly that he felt like it was worth the risk. Even when she let him in on a deep dark secret that she felt would definitely push him away; he still stayed in her corner. Now, he was beginning to feel as if he didn't quite make the right decision. That maybe, just maybe he was wrong for leaving himself out there like that to be hurt.

"Thanks for keeping it a hunnit with me." He looked ahead and took a sip from his cup. Although he was putting up one hell of a front, she could see right through it. They had been married for quite some time, so she knew him inside and out. He was definitely masking his hurt so that she wouldn't see how much her words had devastated him. Even so, she couldn't lie to him when they'd always promised each other before they took their vows to always tell the truth to one another. It was a promise that they both would go on to honor, no matter how much it would rattle the other.

"Of course," she said, swiping away the tears that slipped just over her eyelids, making a funny face as she did so. "We promise one another that we would keep it a stack before we made our union." She held up her delicate hand and wiggled the finger that bared her golden wedding band.

He looked at hers then looked at his, holding the cup of coffee in the opposite hand.

"True dat," Tristan let his hand drop to his side and looked to her. "So what now?"

"What chu mean?" her forehead dipped with crevasses.

"I'm in love with you and you're in love with homeboy." He told her. "That's one hell of a triangle. I'm sure you agree. So what do I do from here? Are we through? What's up?"

Eureka thought on it for a moment and said, "Fear is gon'. I don't know where he is, or if he's every coming back. I can't wait on him. Besides, this is our family, and I'm willing to keep it together no matter what...For Kingston's sake...for all of our sakes." She placed her hand on top of his and rubbed it affectionately.

He sat his cup down on the counter and turned all of the way around to her. "Eureka, you don't love me."

"True. But I will grow to...eventually." She caressed the side of his face while staring into his eyes.

"What if..."

"Shhhhhh," she hushed him by putting a finger to his lips. "We've always knew that it was a chance of what could be, so let's not worry about that until the time comes."

"Have you heard back from anyone yet?" he asked curiously.

"No. Not yet, but I'm sure we'll get a response in the mail any day now." She told him. "I just need to know that you're willing to put what happened then behind us and move forth. Can you do that for me, babe? Can you?"

He looked down at the floor and then back up at her. "Yeah, I can do that. But I want them aware. I don't want them in the dark about it...Especially him."

She took her hand down from his face and turned back around, picking up the cup. She stared ahead at nothing while she took a casual sip of her coffee, thinking. After licking her lips, she said, "Okay. Alright, if that's how you want it then so shall it be."

"Okay then. That's what it is." He took her hand into both of his and kissed it. She cracked a grin. "Look, I'ma hop in the shower, okay?"

"Okay." She nodded. He went to walk away but her holding his hand snagged him. He looked over his shoulder. "I'm sorry about earlier tonight when we were…"

He threw up his hand and said, "Save it. I'm trying to forget that ever happened, so that we can hopefully move on."

"Alright," She released his hand and he went about his business. She went to take a sip from her cup when a voice stopped her.

"I found 'em." The sound of Anton's voice brought her head around to him. He'd just come through the door, toting his motorcycle helmet and stashing his keys inside of his leather jacket.

"Found who?" Eureka frowned.

"Fear," He looked her dead in the eyes and smiled wickedly.

"How? Where?" An intrigued Eureka wanted to know.

"It doesn't matter how, but he's in Cali and I'm going after his black ass." He held up his fit and clenched it so tightly that veins formed around its knuckles.

"Wait a minute, Ant…"

She followed him inside of his bedroom where he was about to get dressed for the night's mission.
****

Tristan stood underneath the spray of the showerhead lathering his body up with soap until he looked like he had been painted white. Right after, he squeezed some shampoo into his palm and massaged it into his scalp. Shutting his eyelids, he planted his hands on the tiled wall and bowed his head. The hot liquid rinsed the shampoo from out of his hair and cascaded down his toned arms and rock hard abs. He swept his hair from off of his forehead and took a deep breath, allowing his thoughts to take him back to the night he had met Eureka. That night he knew that he had met the woman of his dreams. He just didn't know that she was harboring a secret so dark that it would put his life in danger.

Flashback

One Tuesday Eureka found herself at a late night showing of Bruce Lee's The Big Boss. She entered the theater with a big bucket of popcorn and what looked like the world's biggest fountain drink. Usually there was never a soul in sight at the theater, but this particular night there was one dude up in the spot and that was Tristan. This took her by surprise and she found herself occasionally looking back at him. Wondering what he looked like and what kind of person he was. She thought he hadn't seen her checking him out, but she was terrible mistaken.

"Take a picture, it'll last longa." he called her out from the back row when she looked back at him for what he believed was the hundredth time.

"My bad." her face turned red with embarrassment and she turned back around, slumping back down in her seat. She continued to eat her popcorn and indulge in her drink.

Unbeknownst to her, Tristan, who was behind her, had went to reach inside of his bag of popcorn. His forehead wrinkled and he lifted the bag, turning it upside down. When nothing came out he threw the bag aside and looked down to where Eureka was. When he saw that she had a big ass bucket of popcorn, he leaned forward in his seat, a grin fixed upon his face.

"Say, homegirl," he called out to her with a hand cupped around his mouth. She turned around in her seat with a creased forehead, pointing a finger to her chest. "Yes you, I'm willing to forgive you for staring at me with that lustful look in your eyes if you're willing to share some of that popcorn with me."

Eureka looked up at him with an expression of amusement and shock on her face, like the nerve of this nigga. Nonetheless, she was intrigued to find out what kind of nigga that he was so she decided to humor him by taking up his company.

A smiling Eureka waved him over saying, "Come on with yo' bold ass."

Tristan hopped up from out of his seat and darted down the aisle, plopping down in the seat right beside her. He threw his arm over the back of her seat like he was her boyfriend and shit, stuffing his mouth with her popcorn. She looked at his ass with total surprise, not believing the set of balls that he had on him.

"Well, damn, you taking up space with me like you my boo and shit." she looked to the arm he had around the back of her seat and then to him.

"You play yo' cards right and you just may be able to be my queen." he winked at her and threw back a handful of the deliciously hot, buttery popcorn.

Eureka playfully punched him in his arm and said, "Boy, you've got some tongue on you."

"Wouldn't you like to find out." he looked at her grinning. She grinned back and he was floored at how beautiful she was. Biting down on her bottom lip, she marveled his soft brown, bedroom eyes.

"You got a lil' something, something on your mouth there." she brushed the popcorn residue from around his *lips and he smiled, setting off the dimples in his cheeks. For the first time ever she noticed how undeniably handsome he was.*

"Thanks." he told her, still smiling as he extended his hand. "Tristan."

"Eureka." She smiled back, shaking his hand.

Soon after, they settled back down in their seats looking like a couple in the theater, eating out of the same bucket of popcorn and sipping from the same straw of her fountain drink. Once the movie was over they kicked it at Denny's, shooting the breeze and sharing a slice of apple pie and French Vanilla ice cream. Afterwards, Eureka invited him over to her house for drinks. At the time she and Anton were still staying in Fear's house. Down inside of the basement they played pool and had drinks that Eureka occasionally stopped to freshen. As the night winded down she fell asleep on the couch leaving him up by himself, wondering around the basement. He took casual sips from his glass and admired the decor of the basement. Suddenly, his favorite rap song came on and he reverted back to his high school days when he and his little rap crew, The Expertz, use to spit lyrics inside of the cafeteria. Turning toward a sleeping Eureka, he held his drink in one hand while using his other hand to knock on the wall in a pattern. Right when he was about to spit a freestyle off the top of his dome, the wall suddenly shot up into the ceiling startling him. When he turned around he found a secret room with masks and several costumes hanging on the walls. At the back of the room there was a map and a few pictures of people wearing red X's on their faces. It was from this that he assumed that these people had been murdered, especially when he saw a couple of knives, a cachet of guns, and two bulletproof vests lying on the table below.

"Wow," His eyes bulged. He'd just stumbled upon some shit that he totally wasn't expecting. Feeling something cold and hard nudge the back of his skull, his eyes shot to their corners and he lifted his hands up in the air; at the back of him stood Eureka with a Beretta. Her eyes were threatening and her trigger finger was unforgiving.

"Who sent chu, nigga?" she locked her jaws, causing her right temple to pulsate.

"What?" His brows furrowed and he looked nervous. "What do you mean?"

"Wrong answer, dick," She cocked the hammer of her weapon back and applied pressure to the trigger. Behind her Anton came hustling down the steps with a sheathed sword, ready to cut a nigga every way that he could think of. Stopping at the center of the staircase, he grasped the railing and leaped over it. He approached hastily wearing a hard face and a naked upper body, his chest pumping fast as he breathed heavily. Eureka had hit the panic button that was located beneath the edge of the bar top. He was in the bedroom that they had converted into a gym practicing with his sword.

"Fuck is this nigga?" He threw a finger at Tristan looking between him and his big sister.

"Dead, if he doesn't tell me what the fuck I wanna know." her eyebrows arched and her nostrils flared.

"No one sent me after you," he told her the truth. "Are meeting at the movies was fate."

"Fate?" her brows formed a long lump across her eyebrows.

"That's right, fate." he spoke what he believed to be true. "God brought us together, and I'm glad that he did. It was love at first sight."

"Bullshit."

"At least for me it was." he spoke up. "You can't tell me that you didn't at least feel something for a nigga." she was silent, still holding that banger to the back of his dome.

"Okay then, if I'm lying then pop me in my shit right now. Right mothafucking now, kill me goddamn it!" he talked that shit prepared to live or die, whichever hand life dealt him.

"You wan't me to shoot chu?" she asked, making sure.

"Yes, shoot me, fucking shoot me!" he hollered out.

"Shoot this mothafucka, sis!" Anton egged her, looking between them both.

"You heard 'em, shoot me," he cosigned her little brother. "If you know in yo' heart that chu don't feel shit for me after tonight, blow my mothafucking brains out."

"Shoot 'em!" Anton barked on her.

"Shoot me!" Tristan blared at the top of his lungs.

"Alright," Eureka snatched her gun from the back of his head, holding it up at her shoulder and putting the hammer back in place.

Tristan shut his eyelids and took a deep breath, lowering his hands to his sides. If he could he would drop down to his Lord and Savior's feet and kiss them. That's how thankful he was to still have his life right now. He turned around to Eureka to see her stashing her burner at the front of her jeans, pulling her shirt down over it.

Anton stood off to the side of his sister mad dogging her guest for a time before walking off on his bare feet.

"Come on, I'll walk you out." Eureka took him by the hand and led him up the staircase.

That night Tristan convinced Eureka to go out with him again and even got a kiss goodnight. Shortly thereafter,

90

the two of them began a relationship that expanded four years in which they ended up having Kingston and eventually getting married. During this time Tristan and Anton grew pretty close. Their bond wasn't like the youngster and Fear's but they were cordial, if nothing else.

The only reason why Eureka and Tristan had moved into Anton's mansion was so that they could save some money. Although Eureka had plenty of loot stashed for them to buy their own home, Tristan wanted to stack his own dollars and cop the crib himself. Which is why he kept his bouncer gig at the strip club and his little side hustle. He was an Alpha Male and believed in providing and protecting his loved ones. He didn't want his woman lifting a finger. As far as he was concerned, he was the breadwinner and he would take care of his family.

Present

Tristan killed the showerhead's water and stepped out of the tub, grabbing a towel off of the rack. He went about the task of drying his hair and wiping himself down. Having wrapped his towel around his waist, he opened the door and made his exit. There wasn't any doubt in his mind that he was going to do whatever he had to do to keep his family intact, even if it meant killing Fear.

****

"So you're going after 'em?" Eureka questioned her little brother with furrowed brows. She'd just run into the doorway of Anton's bedroom to find him putting on the uniform that he stalked the night in. The nigga looked like he came straight out of a comic book with the shit he had on.

"You goddamn right I'm going after 'em, that son of a bitch killed daddy." He laced up his black leather combat boots.

"Ant, Fear is…"

"What?" he shot to his feet, voice raising a few octaves. "Bigger than me? Stronger than me? Faster than me? More skilled?"

"That's not what I was going to…"

"Well, I've been going through training, Reka, very intense training." Spittle flew from his lips as he jabbed himself in the chest with his finger. "And I'm ready for 'em, I can take 'em! My right hand to God I can beat 'em!" He emphasized, slamming his fist into his palm.

"Anton." Her eyes misted with tears.

Unbeknownst to them Kingston's was standing in the doorway wiping the sleep out of his eyes. He frowned seeing his mother crying. "Don't cry, mommy, everything is going to be okay."

Hearing his young voice drew her attention to him. She walked over to him and picked him up. Looking upon his mother with worry in his eyes, he wiped her face with his little hands as she stared at her little brother like he wasn't doing so.

"Anton…" she called after her sibling, trying to speak some sense into him.

"Don't Anton me; I've been waiting for this day for the past four years." He swore, pulling black leather gloves upon his hands and flexing his fingers. "And his ass is mine." He slammed his fist into his palm, closing his fingers around it. "All mine!"

Eureka sat Kingston down on the floor and stepped to her sibling. "Wait, at least let Tristan go with you."

"Nuh unh," He shook his head no, adjusting his body armor. "This is between me and him. You saw the letter he left me. He called me out, and you know I don't turn down nothing, but my collar."

"But..."

"But nothing!" he cut her short, pointing a finger at her. "If you aren't strapping up to come with me to get at this nigga then I don't wanna hear another word outta you, alright?"

Her forehead wrinkled hearing him talk to her like that. She watched as he turned his back, sliding his handgun inside of its holster where it resided on his thigh. Next, he flipped twin Katanas over in his palms and sheathed them on his back.

"Don't you turn your back on me goddamn it!" she grabbed his shoulder and he whipped around, grabbing her about the throat. He forced her up against the wall with her sneakers dangling like they were hanging from a power line in the middle of the ghetto.

"Don't chu ever in your fucking life put your hands on me again!" he stared into her eyes with fire dancing in his pupils. His jaws were clenched and his chin was crinkled. Tears ran from Eureka's eyes, she couldn't believe her brother would come at her like this.

"Uncle Ant, stop! You're hurting mommy, stop!" Kingston grabbed a hold of his uncle's legs trying to shake him loose from his mother.

"What's gotten into you? I'm your sister, your blood!" she looked upon him like he'd gone mad and he had. Nothing in the world mattered to him more than killing Fear, the man that had murdered his father in cold blood. "You'd put your hands on me? I raised you, you're practically my son." Her eyes soaked her cheeks wet with her heartache and her bottom lip trembled uncontrollably.

"Uncle Ant!" Kingston pleaded for his uncle to stop with his hurting of his mother.

Anton's head snapped down at him. Seeing the hurt and the tears bleeding from nephew's eyes pulled at his heart's strings. He loved him like he shot him out of his own dick. He knew that he admired him and he didn't want him to be afraid of him, or growing up resenting him.

Taking a deep breath, Anton released Eureka of his grasp and she dropped to the floor on her hands and knees breathing hard. With glassy eyes she massaged her sore neck, looking up at her brother as if he was the Devil himself. "Your hatred for him is going to devour your soul; it's going to eat chu alive. You're going to lose yourself if you allow your vengeance to consume you."

Anton pulled a ski-mask with a crooked red S on its forehead over his face and threw his hood over his head. He then turned around to her with unforgiving eyes. "If me sacrificing myself means our father gets to rest in peace, then so be it." He turned back around and made his way towards the door.

"Are you okay, mommy?" Kingston hugged her by the waist, terror in his eyes.

"I'm fine baby." She hugged him with one arm and kissed the top of his head.

The little dude looked from his mother to his uncle then back again.

Eureka stood up as she watched the sway of her brother's shoulders as he headed for the exit. "Anton." She called him back. He stopped and turned around to her. "You're my brother, and I love you more than life its self, but I swear on our father's grave," she shut her eyelids and tightened her jaws before opening them again. She wore a dead serious expression on her face now. "If you ever put your hands on me again, I'ma kill you, nigga." She stated in a cool and calm voice, hot tears slicking down her cheeks.

Tristan bumped into Anton on his way into his bedroom. The young hitter didn't even break his stride when their shoulders collided. Nah, he kept on going like his brother in law wasn't there. With a crinkled forehead Tristan looked back and forth between his wife's tear streaked face and her brother, wondering what the fuck had taken place.

"Reka, what happened?" Tristan embraced his wife, and his son hugged him around the waist.

Eureka pulled back from him wiping the tears that slicked her cheeks. Swallowing, she took the time to answer him, "He went to kill 'em." She whimpered.

"Who? Baby, who is he going after?" he questioned with concern.

Shutting her eyelids and taking a deep breath, she answered him, "Fear."

Chapter 6

Fear pulled up to a motel damn near out in the middle of nowhere and killed the engine of a Canary yellow Dodge Challenger. He'd secured the vehicle on his way over and torched the Mustang that he'd used to kidnap his charge before he made it up north to the big house. They stopped off at a thrift shop and bought some new garments to wear, as well as Raymar a decent disguise. Afterwards, it was In-N-Out Burgers and the road to the nearest shitty motel before they moved out in the morning.

Night had blanketed the city leaving street light posts and stop lights as the only source of lights besides the headlights of the vehicles that occupied the streets. When the headlights went out, Fear took out the keys and tucked them inside of his pocket. Picking up the Raiders baseball cap, he slapped it on his head and adjusted it as he looked himself over in the rearview mirror. He fixed the collar of his jacket and he looked to Raymar, checking out his disguise. He was wearing a wig of cornrows, cubic zirconium earrings and a tank top. He looked nothing like he did earlier when he'd freed him from the confinements of the prison bus.

"Do I look noticeable?" Raymar inquired, turning in his direction to see what he thought of his disguise.

"Hmmmm," Fear placed his hand on his chin and angled his head, forehead wrinkling in thought. He snapped his fingers and said, "I got it." he stuck his hand inside of his jacket and pulled out a pair of reading glasses. He passed them to him and flipped down the visor so that he could give himself a look in the mirror. Once he slipped on the glasses he did just that. "I think that added just the right flare."

"Yeah, this definitely did it, I don't even fucking recognize me." Raymar nodded his approval, turning his head from side to side grinning. He was pleased with his appearance if it wasn't already hard to tell who he was before, then it sure as shit was going to be difficult to identify him now.

Fear grabbed his duffle bag from out of the backseat and turned to Raymar. "Come on, let's go." he swung opened the door and hopped out. He and Raymar kept a suspicious eye out as they headed for the entrance of the motel. Fear pushed open the glass door with his charge coming in right behind him. They approached the front desk where they found a young cat sitting on the stool with his arms folded across his chest, watching the First 48. As soon as a commercial came on he got right down to business with them.

"Hi, how're you doing?"

"Straight," Fear spoke to him. "What do I needa get a room here, boss?"

"Credit card and/ or cash and a picture I.D, my man." he smiled and displayed his teeth, chewing on gum.

"Gotcha." he pulled his wallet out of his back pocket and removed the items that the man had requested. The identification card was a knock off and he had the loot to pay for the stay so he was straight. "Here ya go." he passed the I.D to the clerk who slipped on his glasses so that he could look the fine print over carefully. He removed an ink pen from his breast pocket and pulled his clipboard into him, jotting down the info on a document. While he was writing everything down, he'd occasionally looked up to see Raymar's head on a swivel. After he finished the paperwork, he dropped the ink pen on the desktop and asked them what kind of room they wanted as well as how many beds they required, looking at them like they were gay.

"Two," Fear held up two fingers frowning.

"Aye, aye, there's no judgment here," he held up both of his hands and spun around on the stool, coming face to face with a wall full of keys. His finger scanned down the rows of keys until he found one to a room that had two beds in it. Snatching it off of the hook on the wall, he spun around and tossed the key to Fear. The killer opened his palm and glanced down at the copper key in his palm. "There ya go, room 13 B, you fellas have yourselves a good time."

Fear allowed his eyes to linger on the clerk for a time before telling Raymar to come on. He bopped towards the door with the duffle bag. He crossed the threshold with his charge on his heels.

****

Fear opened the door of the motel to find a modestly furnished room. There was a table and chair by the window which was covered by an off white curtain, two queen sized beds and a flat-screen television set mounted to the wall. He shut the door behind him and tossed his keys upon the table. Afterwards, he and Raymar removed some of their clothing and made themselves comfortable. Fear plopped down on the bed farthest from the door and laid his shotgun down beside him. He picked up the remote control and turned on the television, spotting Raymar at the corner of his eye stripping down to his underwear and wife beater.

"I'ma hit this shower." he informed Fear as he threw a towel over his shoulder and picked up a washcloth.

"That's what's up," the killer folded the flat pillow behind his head so that it would elevate his head. He stared up at the television's screen while flipping through the channels. After not coming across anything entertaining, he decided to see if he would see any reports on the stunt he pulled to spring Raymar from the prison bus. When he didn't see anything on the daring escape, he opted to watch the broadcast that was on. A few minutes later Raymar came out in his wife beater and jeans. Once he finished drying off his neck and shoulders, he went about the task of getting fully dressed. He sat down on the edge of the bed and slipped his socks on one by one.

Knock! Knock! Knock!

"Who is it?" Fear called out, gripping up his shotgun ready to put a big ass hole in a nigga if he was on some bullshit.

"Manager, may I have a word with you please?" the voice came from the opposite side of the door.

Fear sighed and relaxed, stashing the shotgun underneath the mattress. He looked to Raymar who had just lay back on the bed, placing one hand behind his head. He was scoffing his food down like a goddamn dog. Focusing back on the door, the killer approached it and looked through the peephole. Through it he saw someone dressed in all black running full speed ahead at him. His eyelids peeled wide open when he saw him leap up into the air like he was about to do a Lui Kang kick. *Boom!* The door snapped loose from its hinges and it came crashing down. Fear jumped back before he could fall under the mercy of the door. *Oh shit,* read the look on a startled Raymar's face as he jumped up from where he sat on the side of the bed, dropping his half eaten burger on the flat carpet.

"Youuuu." Anton scowled, clenching and unclenching his fists. His Kevlar bulletproof vest rose and fell each time he took a breath. He was hot, on fire, blazing and ready to lock ass.

"Anton?" Fear's brows furrowed and he narrowed his eyelids. He couldn't believe his protégé was standing right there before him.

"Correct, mothafucka!"

Brackkk!

The young nigga fired on his ass, whipping his head around and causing him to stumble back hastily. He bumped up against the nightstand mirror and cracked it into a cobweb when he went slamming up against it. Wincing, he peeled his head up from the ruined mirror and touched the back of his head, looking at his hand which had came away bloody. His vision went in and out as he stared at his stained fingers. Looking beyond them, he saw the youngster following up his attack.

Woop!

Woop!

Swoop!

His fists came lightening fast and Fear moved just as quick, ducking and dodging them. He slipped behind his opponent and pushed him aside, causing him to fall upon the bed. He came back around, lightening fast, just like before, fists and booted feet flying. The killer backed up smacking.

"So this is it, huh?" Fear frowned as his hands swiped back and forth, knocking away the attack before they could make their impacts. Anton was on his ass like stink on shit, keeping the older and more skilled killer on his toes, because one slip up could allow a solid blow to land and seriously injure or kill him. He had trained him exceptionally well and he knew that if it hadn't been for his experience then he was sure that he would have taken him out within the time it took to snap his fingers.

"Unh! Unh! Unh!"

Fear kicked his foot away, smacked his hand down and caught his fist inside of his palm, closing his fingers around it. *Thwrack!* The assassin was caught flush on the jaw and he went staggering backwards. Regaining his equilibrium, he scowled and spit blood aside, wiping his mouth with his fist and leaving a streak of blood along it. When he looked up Anton was flying at him again, the bottom of his boot zooming in on his face. Thinking quickly, he grabbed the younger killer by his ankle and swung his little ass. The youngling shifted himself in the air, flipped over and landed on top of the dresser, unsheathing the Katanas crossed at his back to form an X. He flipped them over in his hands and gripped them tighter. The lighting inside of the room casted off of them, causing gleams to sweep up the lengths of the beautifully crafted blades. Fear's head snapped from left to right trying to find something to defend himself. His eyes zoomed in on a lamp on the nightstand. He was about to snatch it up but it was already too late; Anton was already in motion headed right at him doing fancy maneuvers with the lethal weapons. All he could do was stand there and wait for the deadly blow that would bring his life to an end.

Bloom!

The first blast from the shotgun lifted the little nigga off of his booted feet, slamming him into the dresser's mirror, and cracking it into a cobweb. The Katanas hit the floor one at a time. When he tried to get up, a second blast sent that ass flying halfway across the room. He hit the floor, lying there in pain moaning and groaning.

A frowning Fear looked to where the blasts had come from and found Raymar holding the smoking shotgun at his side. His eyes were staring down at Anton trying to figure out if he was going to live after what he just gave

101

him. He then looked over to the man that had busted his ass out of that bus that was on its way to that prison.

"Thanks." Fear told him with a nod.

"You're welcome. Catch," he tossed him the shotgun and he snatched it out of the air. When he turned back around Anton had disappeared. His heart skipped a beat just as his eyes bulged.

"What the…" Fear ran to the doorway of his room and peered outside, his head snapping from left to right, looking for the man that was trying his damndest to give him a tombstone. "Get the fuck outta here." he said under his breath, not believing that he'd vanished the way that he did. It was like he had taken on the form of vapors and disappeared in thin air. Hearing sirens and seeing their lights ahead, he dipped back inside of the room. "We've gotta get the fuck up outta here and fast." he slipped on his coat and slapped on his Raiders snapback, stashing his shotgun somewhere inside of his coat. Next, he grabbed his duffle bag and threw his head towards the door, signaling for his charge that it was time for them to go. When Fear crossed the threshold, Raymar was right on his heels. The manager and a couple of the motel's guests were outside watching them. Seeing this, Raymar lifted the Baretta that the assassin had passed him before they headed out and cracked off a couple of shots into the air. The loud clapping of the weapon caused the guests to holler and scramble back inside of their rooms.

Fear jumped into his ride, fired that bitch up and sped off, gravel crackling under the tires. Shortly thereafter, the police cruisers were pulling up into the motel's parking lot and hopping out. Unbeknownst to them all, far up in a tree above the motel, sat a fierce young killer. His eyes were casted down at the scenery while his gloved hand felt underneath his bulletproof vest. He grimaced as he felt the soreness in his chest and torso. It was one hell of a close call back inside of the motel room. He'd almost gotten taken out by some snitch ass nigga. He hated to think how his legacy would have read had some shit like that happened.

Looking far up the road, Anton saw the back lights of the vehicle that his adversary drove off in. He hated himself for letting them get away, but he realized that the action that he'd taken was in his best interest. *A good run is better than a bad stand any day,* he thought before he jumped down to the surface. He landed far away from the eyes of the police and the guests of the motel. He fled into the darkness and procured his motorcycle. Once he fired it up all of its colorful neon lights came on and he sped off.

I'ma get cho mothafucking ass next time though. You can count on that, homeboy.

****

Raymar fished out the half of blunt that was left inside of the ashtray and fired it up. He sucked on it and produced smoke that wafted around the confinement of the sport's car. Having indulged, he looked to Fear who was focused on the street. The illumination from the posts flickered on his face, playing tricks with the lighting and making him seem as if he's disappearing and reappearing.

"You alright?" he questioned with concern.

"I'm straight."

"Whoa, that guy back there was fast, I mean real fast," he did fancy martial arts moves with his hands, looking real amateurish and shit. You could tell that this nigga didn't know how to fight for shit. "He was good, too. You could tell that he was exceptionally skilled. It looked like he had you on the ropes, but I get the feeling that you were holding back. Am I right?" he lifted his eyebrows.

"A lil'," Fear nodded.

"I bet chu could you have taken him out like that," he snapped his fingers. "Huh?"

"I wouldn't say that," Fear kept it real. "Although he's not my equal, locking ass with him would not be a walk in the park."

"You guys had a brief exchange, do you know each other?" his brows furrowed.

"Know 'em? I fucking trained 'em."

"Humph," Raymar was surprised to hear this.

Vroooooooom!

The Canary yellow vehicle zoomed up the road with its engine growling like a Rottweiler as it sped along. The lines in the road looked like blurs on the surface they were moving so fast. Fear smiled inside thinking of how far his protégé had came along with his training. He was proud of him, especially having seen how well he'd handled himself back in the motel room. He made him break a sweat; something he hadn't done in a long time. Had he been just a little faster he was sure that he could have gotten the best of him, but thankfully he'd been keeping in shape all of these years.

Round two, lil' brotha, let's see what chu got round two, he thought, shifting the gears and speeding off faster down the naked streets. All that could be seen were the red back lights and the neon headlights of the vehicle.

A couple of hours later

"I had 'em, I fucking had 'em!" Anton punched his fist into his palm and closed his fingers around it. He was now back at his mansion and dressed in silk black pajamas.

"You were close, huh?" The woman that he was talking to through his Blu-Tooth headset asked.

"So close I could reach out and touch the victory." he adjusted the headset as he paced the floor, anger fixed upon his face. "You should have seen his face. He was surprised. He knew that I was a force to be reckoned with. In his heart he knew that I could have possibly beaten him." he held his hands behind his back as he paced the floor, head hung in deep thought. The golden orange flames of the fire licking away at the burning logs inside of the fireplace illuminated the side of him, as he moved back and forth. Someone knocking at the door abruptly stopped his pacing.

"Come in." Anton called out over his shoulder. One of the double doors opened and Tristan slunk in, making his way toward his brother in law. He looked like a dark figure en route towards him within the scarcely light room. As soon as he crossed the path of the fireplace the features of his scowling face and his body were made out under the golden orange illumination of the flames.

Anton turned towards him raising an eyebrow and throwing his head back. "Watts up, big bruh?"

Brack!

The punch Tristan threw sent Anton flying halfway across the room and sliding across the floor. He lifted his head up from the floor smiling and licking his lips, teeth stained red with blood. He wiped the blood from his chin with the back of his fist and slowly scrambled to his feet.

"This is about Reka, right?" He inquired. "I'll be the first to admit I deserved that. Gotta protect wifey right?"

Tristan stood there with the flames of the fireplace flickering off of him and half of his form in the darkness that was the study. His nostrils flared and his chest expanded and shrunk as if he was a raging bull. His fists were clenched and he wanted to throw Anton a beating worthy of a man that had placed his fucking hands on another man's lady, but he decided against it. He knew how much Eureka loved Anton and to do so would put them at odds.

"You put cho hands on my wife again and they'll neva find ya body, mothafucka! I don't give a shit about you being some kind of lethal weapon, or how many niggaz you done killed out here. You lay yo' fucking hands on mine again and I'll fuckin' kill you! I swear on my son's life, I put chu in the fuckin' ground." spit flew from off his lips as he barked his threat, jabbing his finger at his brother in law.

Anton spat blood off to the side and smiled again, "Understood."

With the threat delivered, Tristan turned his back and made his way out of the study, leaving Anton staring at his back. Once he had gone, the young hitter picked up his headset and adjusted it properly on the side of his head.

"Are you alright?" the woman he had been talking to asked.

I'm good. Ain't shit to worry about." He assured her as he turned his attention back to the burning logs. "It was just a lil' family quarrel."

Normally Anton would have put hands on a man that had assaulted him, but he understood Tristan's reasoning for firing on him. Hell, had he been in shoes he probably would have done worse, so he couldn't blame him. He was going to make it his business to apologize to his sister and his brother in law tomorrow morning, but right now he was mentally preparing himself for the fight he'd been gearing up for these past four years. That was the only thing that mattered to him at that moment, everything else was minute.

****

Fear pulled into the woods and hopped out of the car; Raymar was right behind him. The killer made them a campfire and got some old blankets out of the trunk of his ride. Once they made their pallets, he left Raymar at the fire massaging his hands as he tried to keep himself warm. The golden orange illumination of the fire shone on his face as he occasionally blew his hot breath into them. The fire crackled and popped cooking the small branches that had been piled for the fire. When Raymar saw Fear headed back to the opened trunk of the vehicle and then rummaging through it, a line formed across his forehead as he wondered exactly what he was doing. His curiosity got the best of him and he decided to ask him.

"Aye, what're you doing back there?" he got closer to fire and continued to massage his hands. Although his attention was focused on the killer, his hands were still trying to keep themselves warm.

"Nosy aren't we," he came out of the trunk with a length of thin rope, a couple of pots and pans and slammed it shut. "If you must know I'm securing the area. That way we'll know if our lil' friend back there comes looking for us; I'ma set a trap for his lil' ass." Raymar stood hunched by the fire watching Fear slide the pots and pans onto the rope and then secure it around the lower halves of the trees surrounding their sleeping quarters.

Son of a bitch, a smirk emerged on his face as he realized how clever the short muscular man was. If anyone tried to sneak up on them while they were sleeping then the dishes on the rope would act as an alarm. Once Fear had done setting up the outdoor alarm, he snapped his fingers having forgotten something. He dipped back off to the trunk and opened it. Afterwards, he was off to the set the trap that he had told his charge about earlier. Taking his shotgun from out of the car, Fear journeyed back over to the fire where he had made his pallet. He rolled his jacket up to use it as a pillow. Next, he set his alarm on his digital watch for 5: 30 A.M, the crack of dawn. Having done this, he stashed his shotgun underneath a bed of leaves and lay down on his pallet, watching Raymar fiddle with the Beretta that he'd given him. As time wore on he began to blink and found his eyelids growing heavier. His vision became obscured and eventually he shut his eyelids for the last time and sleep whisked him away into a world of dreams.

 ****

 The boiler room was dark and quiet, save for the noisy rats and the occasional trickle of brown water from the rusted pipes that were weaved just below the ceiling. Some of the droplets fell and pelted the young thug's face that was suspended beneath the pipes. Each droplet that hit his cheek slowly began to bring him out of his unconscious state moaning.

 "Uhhhhh, uhhhhhh," he slowly came to, eyelids fluttering like the wings of a moth. He was hanging upside down with his braids dangling. His wrists and ankles were bound by duct-tape and he was rocking back and forth from a shiny, silver chain. Once his vision came into place he looked from left to right, trying to figure out exactly where he was. From the dirty walls, fifthly floor and rusting pipes that dripped brown water, it registered in his mind that he was in the bowels of some sort of tenement. In the shades of the underground dwelling he spotted several rats sitting on pipes and taking up space in crevasses. The small red orbs that was their eyes watching him as he observed them.

Having grown scared, his heart pounded inside of his chest, its beating resonating in his ears. He tried screaming for help, but the bandana that gagged his mouth wouldn't allow any sound to escape. Hearing shuffling around in the darkness, he looked ahead and saw the shadows moving just slightly. At that moment a fat rat came scurrying out and right behind him came Julian. He was wearing a black leather butcher's apron, surgical mask and latex gloves. In his hand was a box-cutter. His thumb pushed its lever up and down, sticking the blade in and out, as he strolled in his capture's direction whistling Dixie. Stopping before the nigga that was hanging from the ceiling, he grabbed a hold of him to stop his swaying back and forth. Once he was still, using his foot, he pulled over an iron chair. He then kneeled down to homeboy that he'd stolen and pulled his gag out of his mouth.

Lil' Fear's eyes were wide with terror and his mouth was trembling. He was breathing in spurts being that he was petrified of what was to come next. Out of all of the shit that he had been through in life, he just knew that he wasn't getting out of this one alive. No one could tell him otherwise.

"Lil' Fear, I'm Julian, pleased to meet cha," the hit-man had pulled the surgical mask down around his neck and introduced himself. "Now earlia when I wus in ya hood, I asked ya about Fear. And like dat," he snapped his fingers, "you went to poppin' dat shit outta ya bloody mouth. You were sucha tough guy den, but now I can see all da bitch bleeding outta ya wit my very eyes. I must say, I am very, very disappointed wit you, bruvh. If you're ya mate's protégé, I would think dat cha would be like his namesake, Fearless." he sat the box-cutter down and pulled a tape recorder from his back pocket, holding it before the young nigga'z eyes. "I'm gonna ask you some questions about cha, homeboy. If I feel like ya lyin', then I'm gonna slice off parts of ya, okay? Okay then." he pressed play on the recorder and stood it up on the seat of the chair. Next, he picked the box-cutter back up and pushed up the lever, exposing the blade. "Just so you know that I mean business and I'm not fucking around here."

"Yarrrr," Lil' Fear screamed at the top of his lungs, squeezing his eyelids shut. His uvula shook at the back of his throat and tears came bursting from around his eyelashes. A long jagged gash opened across his face, running red with blood and getting into his eyes. He blinked his eyelids trying to stop the blood from getting out of eyes, as he continued to scream louder than a mothafucka. Julian cringed and turned his head from the shrilling that was causing his eardrums to ache. Quickly, he picked the gag up from off his neck and stuffed it inside of his mouth. "Now, we shall began," he grabbed his ear and pulled it out as far as he could, lifting the box-cutter and preparing to slice it off if he didn't hear what he believed was the truth. "Is Fear still in Southern California?"

"I don't know, man, I don't know," he managed to say through the gag. He and Julian locked eyes, intensity passing through them both. It appeared that the assassin was trying to decide if he believed the nigga or not. Then it happened all of a sudden...he sliced off his ear.

"Arrghhh!" he danced around on the chain causing it to make its own music as he moved around on it. Blood from the severed ear pelted the floor staining it burgundy. Julian held the ear to his lips and said "Yo, what's up with it, my nigga?" He then gave a throaty laugh, before tossing the severed body part aside. A rat snatched it up as soon as it touched the surface and darted off into the shadows.

Julian went on to ask Lil' Fear a series of questions. When he believed him he spared him the box-cutter but when he didn't he severed something else on his body. Once he couldn't find anything else to hack off of his face, he removed his socks and tossed his sneakers aside. With his ears, nose and eyelids missing, Lil' Fear looked like a bloody faced Mr. Potato Head and he was ready to talk then. He told the hit-man everything that he wanted to know and he allowed him to keep his toes intact. Homie went through about three cassette tapes of recordings getting information from his victim who was relaying all he wanted to know with a weakened, hoarse voice. Julian promised to relief him of his pain once he'd given him what he wanted. When the gangbanger was finally done spilling his guts, the assassin stopped the tape recorder and removed the tape. He stacked the three tapes on top of each other and stashed them inside of the breast pocket of his button up shirt. Next, he slipped the tape recorder into his back pocket and pulled the Desert Eagle from the holster on his thigh, pointing it straight at his forehead.

Lil' Fear shut his eyelids and spoke softly, "Thank you."

"You're welcome."

Blam!

The big gun jerked in his hand and spat an empty shell casing from over his forearm. The casing hit the ground smoking on its side. Chunks of brain dripped from the hollow space in the gangbanger's dome, splattering on the floor. Letting his hand drop down to his side, Julian tilted his head and looked himself over. There were specks of blood all over his clothes and shoes.

"Shit, I've gotta get outta these clothes."

Lil' Fear had given the UK assassin more than enough information than he needed to finally catch up to Fear. He may not have known exactly where to find him but his loved ones sure as hell weren't safe.

CHAPTER 7

The sun seemed to be beaming its brightest that evening. Its rays shined through the partially cloudy sky and warmed the back of the men below. There were seven of them in all, but one of them stood out like a fly in butter milk. This nigga was naked from the neck down and dressed in a pair of black parachute pants. He had a fighter's physique. His body was well defined by muscle and veins. The nasty scars that had amassed over his torso over time gave him character, and told the horrors of some of his most fierce battles and near death experiences. The expression he wore was one of concentration and determination. He stood in a martial arts fighting stance, his eyes bouncing around to all of the hard faces of the men in his presence.

They surrounded him, all six of them. His front, his back, his sides; he was trapped in the center of them. He was ready though. He was born ready. Shit, he was born to kill, that's how he made his living. So this was nothing more than child's play for him. Fists before his eyes, his head snapped in every which direction. His keen eyes taking in the hostile looks of the white garbed, black belts that encircled him, poised to take his fucking head off. They had a katana, dagger, kon, nun chucks, guillotine and saitachis. The men were all still like they were frozen. They were watching him closely and he was watching them. They wanted blood and he wanted their lives. All of their lives.

A bird screeched as it soared high across the sky, setting shit off.

"Ahhhh!" the assailant hollered as he charged forth with his kon. "Ooof!" a kick to the midsection sent his ass back where he came. He hit the ground hard as a mothafucka on his back and rolled backwards, tumbling.

Wop! Wap! Crack!

Anton's fists and bare feet were like blurs in motion. He moved so fucking fast that these niggaz didn't even know that he'd budged. All he saw was that nigga that had murdered his father's face before his maddening eyes. The assault that he dished out gave his opponents expressions of agony, and this brought him great satisfaction. But it was only because he imagined that each and every one of them were his arch nemesis, Fear.

Ping! Ting! Clink! Ging!

The nun chucks, saitachis, dagger and katana hit the ground right after its wielders did. All six men were lying scattered on the ground with bruises and cuts appearing like magic on their faces and shit. With them out of commission, their ally was left to fight Anton head up.

The last men standing circled one another counter clockwise. They were locked into an intense stare down, studying one another carefully and trying to figure out their next moves. The man with the guillotine held his lengthy chain at one end while he winded the deadly end of his weapon up with the other. Abruptly, Anton stopped where he was and narrowed his eyelids at him. The nigga with the guillotine did the same, but kept on winding his weapon up. The young hitter cracked a smile and blew him a kiss. His opponent's face twisted with anger and he unleashed a battle cry, launching the guillotine in his enemy's direction. The guillotine came zooming towards Anton's face. He jumped up in the air and kicked that shit, sending it speeding right back at its welder. The man's face contorted in excruciation as he was cracked dead in the face by his own weapon. The assault left a red bruise behind and sent him sailing back. He hit the surface and flipped over on his stomach, sliding across the ground. Grimacing, he attempted to get up several times, but he had been too weakened by the fight to do so. He tried to push up off of the ground and went slamming back down into it. The defeated man took a last breath and blew debris up in the air.

Anton stood where he was taking a good look at his handiwork, head on a swivel. Satisfied with what he had accomplished, he took a deep breath and walked over to the bottom step of his mansion. After picking up a white towel and wiping himself off, he picked up his check book. He pressed the metal mechanism at the butt of his ink pen that triggered the ball point of it and wrote up a check to pay the men off for the sparring session. As soon as he was finished, he tore the check out of the book and threw it aside. The check went up in the air and came falling down slowly, landing on the chest of one of the sprawled men. Having done this, Anton pulled his location device from out of his pocket. This device was kin to the tracking device that he'd placed on Fear's whip before he fled the motel's parking lot. A smile broadened across his lips when he saw that his enemy and his snitch were still in the same place that they were last night. Now, he was about to get suited and booted and go on his mission. With revenge on his mind, Anton stashed the device in his pocket and jogged up the steps.

****

The sky was a beautiful blue and sunny when Fear's eyelids began twitching and eventually fluttering open. Sitting up, he surveyed his surroundings to find that the camp fire had burned out and smoke was now rising from it. Raymar lay on his side fast asleep, snoring like a momma hog. Fear outstretched his arms and yawned, hearing his bones crackling and popping back into place. He then wiped the scum from the corners of his eyes with a curled finger, licking his lips. Hearing a noise from his left, he looked to find Raymar coming awake stretching and yawning. He looked around also, sticking his hand inside of his shirt and scratching his hairy chest.

"Good morning." he greeted the killer.

Fear threw his head back but didn't say shit. Homeboy had ratted on some made niggaz so he wasn't feeling him at all. As far as he was concerned he wasn't an official nigga so he didn't deserve a warm welcoming. He didn't give a fuck if he did save his life because that's just the type of shit that he was on.

"I'm hungry as a hostage; I was hoping for some breakfast." he smiled in Fear's direction.

"I was hoping to tittie fuck Sanaa Lathan, but let's see who gets lucky first." he gave him a quick fake smile and reverted back to his signature scowl. He felt down in the bed of leaves where he'd stashed his shotgun and frowned when he didn't feel the cold metal that it was made of. With both hands, he swayed back and forth through the brittle leaves but he came up with nothing. His head snapped up to find Raymar looking at him with a crinkled forehead, wondering what the matter was.

"What's the matter?" he worried.

"The shotgun is gone, you got cho piece?"

"Sure, it's right..." his face balled up when he didn't find the Beretta where he'd stashed it for safekeeping. "Its...its gone." he reported, with a face balled tighter from confusion. He could have sworn that he'd hidden it behind the log beside him.

With that said, Fear's head snapped to his left and right; the rope had been severed. A line creased his forehead and he whipped his head back around to Raymar. His eyes zoomed upward above his head and he spotted something shiny that gleamed. He gasped realizing that it was the scope of a sniper rifle. He jumped to his feet running in the direction of Raymar, screaming at the top of his lungs and looking like he was moving in slow motion.

"Get dowwwn!" he yelled, drawing his bowie knife from the worn brown leather holster on his hip. His hand was a flash as he threw it with all of his might. The knife spun around so fast that it was nothing more than a spinning blur. Raymar's eyes snapped open as wide as they could and his mouth stretched open to its limits. His heart thumped inside of his chest, seeming as if it was about to burst at any moment then. Shutting his eyelids tightly, he swallowed the lump in his throat and hoped that the knife would bring him a quick death. The handle of the knife struck him right in his forehead and he went sailing back to the ground just as a chirp sounded off. A moment later a bullet struck the surface sending debris into the air.

Raymar lay on the ground wincing and moaning, a sore lump growing on his forehead. Fear's eyes zoomed in on his charge and he was thankful that he was able to knock him off of his feet before that bullet splattered his ass. His head snapped around and he looked up, zeroing in on the sniper. He narrowed his eyelids when he realized that it was Anton. Although he was angry a crooked smile infiltrated his lips. For some odd reason he felt a sense of pride surge throughout his body. It was probably because the young gunner was his little nigga, his student, his protégé, his successor, the heir to his throne of certified head buster.

Persistent fucker aren't we? I taught chu well, junior, he thought until Anton started blazing at his mothafucking ass, too. Retreating back to his vehicle, he snatched up his bowie knife and took cover behind the Challenger, using it as a shield. He looked underneath the car and saw that Raymar was coming to, eyelids fluttering open as he moved his head from left to right.

"Stay down behind that log, he can't hit what he can't see," he pulled his head back from underneath the vehicle and sat with his back against the side of it. He shut his eyelids and repeated to himself rapidly. "Come on Fear, think, think, think." An idea hit him like a hammer hits a nail on the head at that moment and his eyelids snapped open. Swiftly, he opened up the driver side door and crawled inside over the driver seat. He picked up the slingshot that Raymar was playing around with earlier and slithered back out of the car, slamming the door shut quietly. Down on his knees, he sheathed his knife and began gathering rocks. Once he felt that he had a sufficient amount, he took a look underneath the car again looking for his charge. He frowned up once he saw that he was gone. Right then, he heard huffing and puffing and hurried footsteps coming from his right. He peeked over the hood of the Challenger and saw who he was looking for zig zagging through the woods holding his arms over his head, trying to guard his crown from a hot one. Across the woods and yards away, he found Anton behind the trigger of his sniper rifle trying his damndest to draw a bead on him.

"Didn't this stupid mothafucka hear me? I said to stay yo' ass behind that fucking log!" he gritted and scowled. "Oh, shit!" his eyebrows lifted and his mouth formed an O when he noticed the direction that Raymar was running in. It was the same space that he had set that trap last night. *Fuck,* he thought seeing the rope capture his ankle and snatch his ass up into the air, leaving him dangling from a tree. His head snapped over to Anton and he loaded the slingshot, seeing him about to take the kill shot.

"Hellllllp, helllllllp me, pleeease," Raymar's dumbass rocked back and forth, trying to lift up and undo the rope that was strangling his ankle.

Sniktttt!

Fear drew his blade from where it was sheathed and ran in the direction of his charge. His cheeks swelled and deflated as he breathed huskily. Snatching the knife from between his teeth where he had put it, he flipped the handle over in his hand and launched that bitch. *Whook! Whook! Whook!* The knife seemed to spin in slow motion en route to its target. Across the way, Anton slightly jerked as he pulled the trigger of his rifle and it recoiled, sending an empty copper shell casing flying from its side. The piping hot bullet zeroed in on its target's head while the spinning knife was headed for the rope, just seconds behind the shot that was fired.

"Hollllly sheiiit!" Raymar's eyelids shot wide open just as his mouth did. To himself he sounded like he'd been chopped and screwed, like those songs by DJ Screw. His neck twisted from left to right seeing the knife, which was spinning like a helicopter propeller heading for him, and the sharp copper slug twisting in his direction. Realizing that his life was hanging in the balance, he squeezed his eyelids shut and wrapped his arms around his head. He prayed for the mercy of God Almighty to save his ass because if He didn't then it was grass. The swirling blade sliced the rope in half and he went hurtling towards the surface. The bullet missed his head by an inch, burying into the ground.

"Ughhhh!" his face balled up upon impact to the ground. He turned over on his side grimacing but thankful that he was alive. Fear smiled victoriously and ducked back down beside the Challenger, preparing his slingshot. Once it was good and ready, he came running from alongside the vehicle with one eye shut. He pulled the rubber band back containing the rock and launched it, sending it zooming towards its target. *Ping!* The impact of the rock knocked off the scope of the rifle causing Anton's head to snap up from it. By the time he looked up a second rock was slamming into his chest. He grimaced and howled, grabbing the sore area where he was struck. *Crack!* A third rock impacted his forehead, snapping his head back and dropping him from out of the tree. He went freefalling toward the ground, making a loud thud when he hit the surface.

Heart pumping, adrenaline coursing like mad, Fear cautiously approached a sprawled Anton. Stopping along to pick up a long crooked branch, he took it into both hands. He got about five feet upon him before poking him with it. When all he did was nudge, he felt a bit bad for having killed him. Although he knew that it was either him or himself in that time that he was blazing at him, that didn't stop the heartache he felt from having kill the young man that he loved like a younger brother. Tossing the branch aside, he advanced in Anton's direction until he was right up on him. Kneeling down to his knee, he went to scoop him into his arms and that's when he got the surprise of a lifetime: a poisonous dart to the chest. His forehead wrinkled and he looked down to find it in his stomach. He looked back up to find Anton with a tranquilizer gun aimed at him. Swiftly, he smacked the thing out of his hand and took off running, stumbling occasionally as the dart was slowing him down. Every so often he would look over his shoulder to see if his attacker was still on him and he was, reloading the gun as he went along. Fear kept running. When he looked ahead and saw Raymar there, he motioned for him to run but the stupid mothafucka kept standing there. Anton stopped and gripped the gun with both hands, aiming and pulling the trigger. The gun made a funny noise and the dart spat out, twisting in the air while en route. It found its home in its target's back. Fear grimaced and veins bulged in his temples. He staggered along trying to pull the dart out feeling woozy. He saw double and even triple before his eyes. Swinging around, he met the shooter before crashing to the ground on top of several dead leaves. Anton approached loading another dart into his weapon; he leveled it at his prey as he stood over him.

"See you when you wake up, homeboy." his hand jerked when he pulled the trigger and sent his old sensei into darkness. His head snapped up and he spotted Raymar looking shook. His eyes were wide and his mouth was hanging open. The nigga had been caught seeing that shit when he should have been using that time to get the fuck up out of dodge.

"Shit." he cursed before taking off running through the woods. He stumbled and fell but got right back up, hauling ass. Seeing this, Anton hurried up zip cuffing his mentor's wrists and ankles to make sure that he didn't get away. Afterwards, he recovered the crooked branch that Fear had and hopped upon his motorcycle which he had camouflaged under a pile of leaves. Revving up the sexy machine, he zoomed through the woods with a tight grip on the branch. The trees became blurs he was moving so fast, leaving debris and dead leaves in the air.

"Haa! Haa! Haa! Haa!" Raymar breathed heavily, as he moved swiftly through the woods. His body was hot and he was sweating like a runaway slave, chest jumping up and down. Occasionally, he'd glance over his shoulder, and when he did, it seemed like the young killer was getting closer and closer, until he was damn there on top of him. Anton swung the branch at his legs and flipped his bitch ass. He went up into the air and came down on his back, harder than a bitch. He slowly picked his head up from the surface wincing and feeling dizzy. Before he knew it the nigga on the motorcycle was speeding back in his direction, branch extended at his side. Raymar struggled to get up having not found his wit or his equilibrium. By the time he was on all fours and looking up, the branch was going upside his head and he was meeting the same darkness as Fear.

****

A wincing Fear blinked his eyelids as he slowly came out of his induced sleep. He groaned softly looking around trying to figure out where he was. His vision came into focus and he realized that he was lying on the backseat of his own car. He went to move his arms and legs and found that they were bound. Looking down he saw that his ankles were wearing zip-cuffs. That's when he looked up and saw the back of someone's neck. It wore a fading tattoo on the side of it, Eureka. It was Anton that had kidnapped him. Fear bent his legs all of the way back to his behind and slipped the knife that he had stashed there out. Triggering the weapon's blade, he went about to the task of cutting himself free of his restraints.

"Where's Raymar?" he called up front to Anton.

Anton adjusted the rearview mirror so that he could see Fear in the backseat; the killer was just sitting upwards.

"Heyyyyy, Sleeping Beauty," Anton greeted him with a smile, acting real jovially like. "If you're looking for yo' snitch ass homeboy, I stashed his ho ass in the trunk. Don't worry about him 'cause I ain't letting nothing happen to that one there. He's worth too much mothafucking money for me to let something happen to him before he lands into paying hands, ya feel me? Now you on the other hand," he scowled into the rearview mirror so that he could see him. "You and I have a score to settle. I'm gonna take you somewhere where no one can hear you scream, you black hearted son of a bitch!" he slammed his fist against the steering wheel in a rage, tears flowing down his face rapidly. He didn't care if his enemy saw them because it was because of him that he was shedding them. "You took him; you took him away from me…From Reka, from us! Our! Fa-therrr!" he roared, speckles of saliva clung to the rearview mirror and his breath fogged it up. His shoulders rose and fell as he took husky breaths, trying to calm down. He wiped his spilling eyes with the back of his gloved hand and then sniffled.

"I know and it's something I gotta live with everyday, lil' brotha." he dropped his head feeling bad for having to cause someone that he loved so much pain and turmoil. It was obvious that his father's death had taken its toll on him and was eating him alive, each and every day. "Again, I am sorry. I know it don't mean much to you though, right? You want revenge, am I right?"

"You mothafucking right I want revenge, nigga," he nodded and glanced up at the rearview mirror. "Reka took out momma for hers and I'ma take you out for mine. Once this is over I can get back to living my life."

"Just like that, huh?"

"Yeah, mothafucka, just like that." he scowled harder and gripped the steering wheel with both hands.

"I Griff you, youngin', do what chu gotta do, 'cause I for damn sho' am."

When he said this, Anton looked up into the rearview mirror to see Fear's arms swinging up from around his back. His right hand held tight to a small, sharp ass knife with a razor's edge.

When he went to lunge at Anton, the young nigga quickly swerved his car to the left sending his head slamming into the back window. The window cracked into a spider's cobweb and he winced, dropping the handy weapon. He fell back against the seat moaning and trying to focus his eyes, his head bleeding. He bit down on his bottom lip and turned to the side, seeing his knife on the floor. Grasping it, he made to stab his mark in the neck but another swerve sent him to the right and caused him to drop his weapon again. Fear squared his jaws and with a growl, he lunged forth. Anton slammed on the brakes and sent his mothafucking ass flying through the windshield. He exploded through the windshield bringing shards along with him, hitting the surface rolling with broken glass until he eventually stopped. He lay there in the middle of the street with his chest rising and falling. The killer was still but he was breathing. His body was also hurting for that matter.

Anton threw the car in park and sat there for a time, staring at Fear.

"Aye, Heyyyyy, what the fuck is going on out there?" There was thumping and bumping inside of the trunk as Raymar was punching around in it.

"Shut cho bitch ass up, nigga," Anton called out over his shoulder as he unbuckled his safety belt and opened the driver side door. Swinging the door open, he stepped outside one booted foot at a time. He slammed the door shut and headed over in his former teacher's direction.

Fear was lying stiff as hell in the middle of the street with broken glass littering him and the space surrounding him, when Anton cautiously approached him. For all Anton knew the mothafucka was playing possum and he wasn't for any surprises. He kicked him twice but he didn't budge. It was then that he believed that he was dead. He stood over him taking a deep breath, relieved that he'd finally avenged his father's murder. Abruptly, Fear's eyelids snapped open and he swung his foot around, sweep kicking his former student off of his feet. The young killer hit the surface hard and bumped his head. Twisting his head from left to right, he moaned and blinked his eyelids. His vision came in and out of focus as his brain tried to establish exactly where he was. Narrowing his eyelids, he saw someone out of focus go up into the air, leg extended. His vision came back into place and he found that it was Fear, doing a mothafucking leg drop on that ass.

"Ahhhhhhh!" The killer's face was tightened at the center as he roared, coming down hastily with his leg aimed for the little nigga'z throat. Anton moved out of the way at the last minute and he came down hard on his ass, wincing. The younger assassin came up from behind him, locking his neck in a chokehold and pulling him to his booted feet. Fear staggered backwards while trying desperately to pry his muscular arms from around his neck. They were like twin pythons squeezing him tightly to cut off his oxygen supply. Veins bulged at his forehead and neck, as he was turning red. His became teary and he went flying back hastily, bumping up against a tree. Thinking quickly, he stomped Anton's foot. When the youngster went to grab for his foot that left his face open and Fear took the advantage. Whipping around, he went to work on Anton's face. He swung his fists back and forth across his jaw, whipping his head from left to right. It looked like the younger killer was through until he blocked the next attempt at knocking him out and punched him flush in the mouth, snapping his head back. When Fear brought his head back down his teeth were stained red, his lip had been split as a result of the assault. He followed up with hard slugs to the jaw that sent speckles of blood flying everywhere. Once he went to go kick him he caught his leg, and that's when he went to punch him. Fear grabbed the young nigga by his wrist and twisted his arm around, causing him to wince. He then brought his leg over him and jumped up into the air, bringing his leg down hard on his back.

"Oooof!" Anton lay on the ground with the weight of his mentor's leg on his back, aching like a son of a bitch. He busted his mouth on the asphalt. Fear took his wrist by both hands and gritted as he attempted to yank his fucking arm out of its socket.

"Grrrrr!" the veins rolled up Fear's neck and temples, his arms slightly vibrated as he tried to pull the limb loose. Anton squeezed his eyelids shut and bit into the street, refusing to beg for mercy. And that's when it happened to him. What's that? His arm came out of place.

"Arghhhh!" Anton hollered out, eyes turning glassy from the excruciation. Fear released him and quickly got to his feet, ready to get it in. "Ssssss, arghhh…" The young gunner got to his booted feet with his ruined arm dangling at his side. It had been popped out of its socket and there wasn't no way in hell that he could lock ass with Fear now. Even so, he was determined to fight him with one arm if need be. Holding up his gloved fist, he slid his booted feet into a fighting stance.

"Heart, you've always had it, kid. That's why I trained you; same as me." Fear lifted his scarred and calloused fists, tucking his chin to his chiseled chest. "No retreat…"

"No surrender." Anton finished his mantra and squared his jaws, clenching his fist tighter.

"You realize that you can't win this, right?" Fear told him this while staring dead into his unforgiving eyes.

Anton spit out a slither of blood over his shoulder. "We'll see, nigga."

"See we shall." his eyebrows arched and his nostrils flared.

"Indeed." his eyebrows arched and his nostrils flared, too.

Fear and Anton were so engrossed with their fighting that they weren't aware of the police cruiser flying up the street, siren blaring. The possibility of going to jail never invaded their minds. Nah, they were solely focused on trying to take one another out.

Anton moved like the speed of light dodging the fists and booted feet of Fear, barely escaping his lethal attack. It wasn't until he ducked and smacked his fist away that he was punched square in his face by him. The vicious blow threw his head back. He stumbled backwards but he caught himself, charging back into the fight. When Fear saw him coming at him, he stuck his thumb into the loop at the back of his jeans and brought his fist before his eyes. He did this so the fight would be evenly matched and there would be no mistaken who the victory was in this glorious battle.

Pact! Pact! Pact! Thack!

Fear bobbed and weaved, smacking his opponent's fist down when they came near his face or body. Both men were sweating profusely and breathing heavy as fuck. Anton tried to kick Fear and he kicked his leg away. His fist came flying at him and he smacked that away from his grill.

That's when he got a big surprise; his protégé punched him the face with the fist of the arm that he thought he'd pulled out of its socket. Fear saw a flash of white and his face twisted, as he stumbled backwards. Anton smiled deviously and moved in on the man that had taught him the bulk of all there was to know about murder. The seasoned assassin danced on his feet and hunched over, as his student worked him. His fists pumped back to back pummeling his mid section. He brought up his savage blows, punishing his chest before whipping his head from left to right. With that, Anton jumped into the air swinging his leg around and uncoiling his foot. Dazed, Fear stood up on his feet, head bobbling and arms at his sides. His knees buckled like he was about to fall but he managed to stay upon them, seeing his rival in mid air. He saw him whipping around three times, bringing his foot around on some Jean Claude Van Damme shit.

Blowl! Blowl! Blowl!

Even the Round House kick had the impact of three as it was brought across his jaw. The force of the blow threw Fear to the right and he went crashing on his side, blood running from his mouth onto the street. He lay there breathing awkwardly, chest filling and dropping with every breath that he took. His eyelids were slits, revealing nothing but whiteness in their openings. The police cruiser was almost at the scene when Anton pulled the burner from out of the holster on his hip. Stopping before his enemy, he leveled the gun at his melon and scowled hard.

"This is for my father." he told him as his finger curled around the trigger.

Pop!

"Drop it, asshole!" a voice rang out from the side of Anton. He didn't need to turn around to know that it was the police. One of them had licked off a warning shot in the air but he was sure that they'd put one in his noodle if he didn't comply with their order.

Anton clenched his teeth hard as fuck being that he was in a blind rage. His finger was right there on the trigger of his Death Dealer and all he had to do was give it a little squeeze. The thought of offing Fear and letting the pigs take him out along with him ripped back and forth across his mental. He heard the cop commanding him to drop his gun repeatedly but he pushed them out of his mind until they became inaudible. Inside of his head he and his enemy were the only ones there in the middle of the street. The background was black and there was a spotlight on them. He could see himself watching from afar, his view like a bird high up in a tree. He was right there, so close. He could literally reach out and touch his revenge. I mean, actually grasp it and hold it inside the palm of his hand. The only thing that was stopping him was he still had Eureka and Kingston to look after. If it wasn't for that then he would have blown that nigga Fear's head off right there in the middle of the mothafucking street.

Anton tossed his weapon aside, hearing the metal clasp as it hit the surface. Still staring down at Fear, he took a deep breath.

"You either have nine lives, or a very fucking lucky rabbit's foot."

"Get down on ya knees and place your hands behind your head!" the cop commanded.

Anton bent down to his knees and placed his hands behind his head like The Ones had ordered.

"Don't move!" The approaching cop holstered his gun and pulled out his handcuffs. While he moved to restrain the suspect his partner kept his weapon trained on him, both hands gripping his sidearm.

"Fuck you!" Anton hurled, he hated the police almost as much as he hated Fear.

CHaptER 8

Forty minutes later

Anton, Fear and Raymar rode in the back of a police van chained the fuck up. The vehicle rocked back and forth as it was driven down the paved road, causing the chains that were restraining its passengers to rattle. Raymar's eyes were trained on Anton who was mad dogging Fear with a tight jaw. All Fear was doing was lying back against the wall of the van, his eyes watching his former student curiously. Suddenly, he leaned forward and rested his hands on his knees. They held one another's glare, never breaking eye contact. Abruptly, Anton lunged forwards but the chains retrained him, rattling and coming just inches of his rival's face. He sneered and snapped his teeth at him trying to bite his fucking face off. He looked like a beast confined in a cage, with all of the spittle flying off of his lips.

The younger killer settled down and let his hands drop to his sides, nostrils flaring, chest heaving. His hateful eyes stayed on the man that had brought him under his tutelage. He wanted so badly to break the restraints of those chains that bonded him and get a piece of his ass, but he knew that at that time he would have to wait. His main concern now was getting out of that van before they made it down to the precinct.

"I know you'd come for me, there wasn't any doubt in my mind." Fear stated honestly. "You're stubborn and vindictive. You'd never let what had happen die, and for that matter, neither would I had it been my father. You and I," he motioned a finger between them. "We're one in the same; cut from the same cloth, but there's something you needa understand about this here murder shit…" he leaned forward, his soulless eyes staring into those equal to his

131

own. "Some of us are born to do it while others have been trained."

"I'm going to take everything you have ever taught me, my nigga, and I'm gonna crush you with it. You hear me, homeboy? We'll see who is the realest killa is then." his eyes burned with fire and determination. He held up his clenched fists and gritted so hard that the muscles in his jaws pulsated.

Fear cracked an amused smirk. "You really think you can beat me, huh?"

"You goddamn, right? And what the fuck are you smirking at, pussy?" he shot back heatedly.

"I guess you figga you had me dead to rights back there?" he threw his head slightly to the double doors of the van.

Again the vehicle rocked back and forth as it journeyed, causing the chains of its prisoners to rattle.

Raymar's head snapped back and forth between the two professional hit-men. He was intrigued about what their beef was about. He also found it interesting that the man that had busted him out of that prison bus had groomed the other man to be a killer, and now he intended to kill him as soon as time permitted it.

"You goddamn right I did." Anton assured him with a glare.

"I'll allow you to think that, I coulda taken yo' lil' punk ass out any time I felt like it." Fear spoke sincerely.

"What I wouldn't give to be locked inside of a cage with you for five minutes."

"Be careful what chu wish for, champ, you may just get it."

Boom!

Something crashed into the side of the police van flipping that mothafucka over. It went tumbling down the street before skidding on its rooftop and coming to a stop. There was moaning coming from inside of the confines of the wrecked vehicle, niggaz were sprawled out at funny angles looking like they were either dead or stirring awake from their sleep. Anton threw his head back and slowly peeled his eyelids open, looking at Fear and Raymar. Raymar was knocked out cold while Fear's eyelids were flickering white and there was bleeding at the side of his head. Hearing hurried footsteps at the back of the van, Anton looked to the double doors. There was talking at the rear and then someone yelling for someone else to step back. Once they obliged, some kind of tool was used to snatch the locks out of each of the double doors. The double doors came open shining light inside of the van. Anton and Fear looked up narrowing their eyelids. All they could see were two silhouettes with a florescent light dawning on their backs. They couldn't make out their faces but they were packing AK-47s. The shapes of the weapons made this apparent.

"Who...who is that?" Fear grimaced.

"The cavalry, asshole," Anton looked to him with a smile. He then turned his right ear toward him, tapping the ear bud that was sitting snuggly there.

The smaller of the silhouettes climbed inside of the van with a pair of bolt-cutters. Although there was a black bandana masking the lower half of his face, Anton could make out exactly who it was approaching them. They were wearing a Dickie suit and slinging the strap of the assault rifle over their shoulder, gripping the bolt- cutters with their freehand.

"Eureka." Fear's forehead creased seeing the young lady that he'd fallen in love with so many years ago. He couldn't believe his eyes. It had been so long that things seemed surreal right then. But it was true. It was Eureka, right there in the flesh.

"Is that brotha in law behind you, sis?" Anton held a hand over his brows and narrowed his eyelids, peering out into the light to see who had helped his sister rescue him.

"Yeah, it's me, baby boy." Tristan answered, he was suited and booted just like Eureka.

"My nigga," Anton said, sounding like Denzel Washington in *Training Day*. "I knew you were gonna roll."

"Fa sho'," Tristan nodded. "We're fam."

Eureka cut the chains that restricted her brother. As soon as he was let loose, he snatched the AK-47 that was hanging from her shoulder, cocked that bitch, and pointed it at Fear. The season assassin mad dogged him, squaring his jaws and causing his entire head to quiver. This nigga wasn't scared of a mothafucking thang.

"Ant, nooo!"

Blatatatat!

Eureka lifted the spitting assault rifle up from Fear as he was turning his face. Large holes blew through the side of the van and the sun's rays shone through them, putting golden spots of light on Anton and Eureka.

"Fuck you doing!" Anton growled and shoved her aside, nostrils expanding and shrinking. His chest swelled and fell with each breath that he took.

"You can't kill 'em." she looked at him with pleading eyes.

"Why in the fuck not?" he stepped into her face, their noses touching one another. She didn't back down.

134

Her eyes took on a dangerous look and she gritted, balling her fists firmly.

"You've always talked about killing his ass honorably, right? Guns aren't the way, these are, lil' brotha." she lifted her fists.

Anton shut his eyelids and took a deep breath, nodding his approval. He knew that his sister was right. After passing the AK-47 back to his sister, he took the bolt-cutters from her and snapped the chains from Fear's wrists and ankles. A line formed across his forehead and he looked up at the young gunner, massaging his wrist. The expression on his face was one of surprise as he couldn't believe that he'd just set him free.

"We're gonna settle this one way or another." Anton began. "Meet me at the mountains where you trained Reka and I; eight o'clock sharp. We fight 'til the death."

Tatatatatatatatat!

The sudden burst of gunfire caused everyone to look alive. Anton looked over his shoulder and Tristan was gone.

"Babe, took out the cops...they saw your face." Eureka reported.

"Right." He whipped back around to Fear.

"I'll be there." the killer spoke, letting him know that he'd be there at the mountains for their death match.

"Uhhhhhh!"

The moaning of an injured man brought their attention to over their shoulders where they found Raymar coming to, shaking off the dizzy spell from the crash.

"We're taking him." Anton started in Raymar's direction.

"Why?" Eureka wondered.

"He's a payday, worth half a mill easy." he snapped Raymar's chains with the bolt-cutters and yanked him to his feet. Wagging his finger into his face he said, "As of now you're with me. You move when I move and you do as I say. You try to run and I will gun you the fuck down, I swear before God. Homie that wants you doesn't give a fuck if he gets you dead or alive. Do you understand me?" he glared at him with eyes that told him that he would make good on his threat if he chose to defy him.

Raymar didn't say anything as he stared at Fear and he stared back. He was looking at him like *I know you just not gone let this nigga steal me like this*. Understanding what this look was interpreting, he nodded and assured him that he wasn't about to let it go down like that.

"Let's go, let's move!" Tristan hollered out as he came running around the van. He stepped into the doorway of the wrecked vehicle. "One time is on the way."

While he was saying this, Eureka and Fear were locked into a gaze. They both wanted to say something but their thoughts wouldn't roll off of their tongues. Their eyes communicated one thing that they didn't have to say: they were still very much in love with one another. Even after all of these years. Even after all of the deceit, lies, murder and bullshit that had happened between them, they were still head over hills. She hated him for how she felt about him after learning he had murdered her father and he hated himself for ever having to pick up a gun, because ultimately his life of crime lead him down the road of a hit-man.

When she stopped her brother from murdering him out it wasn't really because it wasn't the honorable thing to do. Nah, she didn't want him to kill the love of her life and she didn't want him to die before she had the chance to tell him something that was very important to her. The secret was eating her alive and she knew that if she didn't get it out that her entire being would be devoured.

"Fear." she called for his attention.

He threw his head back like *What's up?*

"I…"

"Baby, come on!" Tristan cut her short with his calling of her. She looked to him and he was standing outside the van with an AK-47. Anton stood beside him with a firm grip on the back of Raymar's neck. The young gunner's prisoner was wincing and squirming from all of the pressure that was being applied to his neck.

Police car sirens were blaring from a distance. This had the three men on high alert and they were ready to get the fuck from off of the scene asap.

"Baby?" Fear frowned hearing the man that his lost love showed up with saying this. He looked between them both looking for an explanation.

Eureka looked back at him and nodded like *Yeah, he called me baby.*

"Let's go!"

With that, Eureka came hurrying out of the van and jumping down into the street.

"Go ahead, I'll catch up." Tristan told her, once she and Anton had ran off, he turned back around to Fear. Bracing the stock of his AK-47 against his shoulder blade, he aimed it at the nigga that was standing between him and the heart of his wife. An expressionless Fear stared blankly at the man that had that choppa on his ass. He was either going to do him in or he wasn't. It didn't make any difference to him. Ever since he chose his way of life he knew that he was living on borrowed time and was willing to accept that.

"You love her, huh?" Fear wanted to know.

"Yep."

"Well, do it then…Shoot. Shoot me!"

Pop this nigga, Trist, pop 'em! This mothafucka is going to destroy yo' family; break up a happy home. You tryna be some weekend dad if Eureka decides to take up time with this fool? Nah, nah, nah, bad as I want to, a nigga can't do it like that, he thought to himself, finger settled on the trigger. One squeeze and he could light Fear's ass up like Christmas trees on December 25th.

As bad as Tristan wanted to shoot Fear he couldn't bring himself to do it. This was not the way that he wanted to win Eureka over. Truthfully, he wanted her to somehow come to the conclusion that he was the man that she actually wanted to be with. He didn't want to get her to choose to be with him through some form of deceit. That wasn't his way at all. Nah, he wanted to win his wife's heart fair and square.

"Grrrrrr, fuck," Tristan suddenly took the choppa down and slammed his fist into the van's door repeatedly. He was mad as a mothafucka that he couldn't bring himself to pop the nigga that had staked claim over his wife's heart. He knew that he may hate himself later for not going along with his first mind, but he was going to let this shit ride anyway.

For a time Tristan and Fear were staring into one another's eyes, unflinchingly. The sudden sound of a honking horn stole the Dominican man's attention and he went sprinting off, toting his AK-47.

****

Tristan retreated back towards the truck that he and Eureka had crashed into the police van with. It was a Nissan Pathfinder with a reinforced crash-bar. Running forward, he passed Eureka who was on Anton's motorcycle. They'd recovered it from the tow truck that the police had loaded it on to be carried off. Eureka revved up the beautiful ebony machine and sped off, motioning them on to follow after her. Tristan climbed into the Nissan and tossed his assault rifle into the front passenger seat. In the backseat he found Anton and Raymar having adjusted his rearview mirror.

"You good?" Tristan asked him speeding off, one hand gripping the steering wheel.

"I'm money, big bro, you know me." Anton looked beside him where he found a duffle bag labeled police. Unzipping it, he found all of his weapons as well as the rest of his belongings. Right after, he glanced back up to the front, seeing the back of Tristan's head. At that moment he was pulling the bandana down from over the lower half of his face. Unbeknownst to him, he had been watching what he was doing through the rearview mirror the entire time.

"We caught up with The Ones the moment you hit Reka up." he informed him. "You know we got those radars, scanners and police radios on deck. We picked up right where the pigs were when we listened in on them talking to the dispatcher and shit."

"G looking, bro bro." he nodded his appreciation.

"Don't mention it, homie, we family…" he stole a glance through the side view mirror to see if The Boys were on his ass. They weren't though. "Family looks out for one another, right?"

"Sho' ya right."

For a time they rode in silence. Anton stared out of the back window while Raymar had begun to doze off, head nodding.

"Why didn't chu just pop 'em?" Anton spoke again.

"Huh?" Tristan frowned through the rearview mirror.

"I said, 'why didn't you just puff that nigga Fear's wig out back there?'"

"I want yo' sister, but I want her to choose to be with me," he admitted. "I don't want her with me 'cause she can't be with him, ya feel me?"

"Honorable man, I can respect that." he nodded his understanding. "The difference between you and I is, I like to win. I don't care about how I gotta go about doing it either, just as long as I'm the victor."

"Salute."

Flashback

That day wasn't Tristan's first time killing a mothafucka. He'd actually caught his first body when he was just eight years old. He'd been awakened out of his sleep by his drunken father beating the living shit out of his mother. Creeping out of his bedroom, he made his way inside of his parents' bedroom and got his father's .44 magnum revolver from underneath the mattress. He was very familiar with the pistol. This was because his father had taught him how to shoot it a couple of years prior. Having checked the chamber of the shiny, chrome weapon and seeing that it was fully loaded, he closed it as quietly as he could. Taking the heavy steel into both hands, he moved out of the bedroom, as silent as the grave. He moved down the dark corridor with the light from the kitchen shone on his face and body.

"Bish, you eva tell me stop drinkin', I'ma muddafuckin' grown as main." Roberto slurred as he stared down at Maria, his wife and his son's mother. He had a telephone cord wrapped around his knuckles. His face and arms were sweaty and his chest was puffing up and down. His wife beater was clinging to him because of his perspiring. The crazy Spanish nigga had just finished whipping on his woman. "Me da main of dese house, me!" he smacked his hand up against his chest.

"I sorry, papi, I sorry," Maria was balled up on the floor in a fetal position. She was sweated and there was red streaks decorating her limbs. The cord she'd been beaten with had cut through her skin and caused her bleeding. Lying beside her was a half broken bottle of Jack Daniel's, its dark alcohol soiled the linoleum.

"Me don't think ju is, bish, but chu will be." he drew back his hand to continue beating her mothafucking ass.

Her eyes bulged and she screamed hysterically, veins bulging at her temples and up her neck, *"Ahhh! Ahhhh! Ahhhhhh!"*

"Papi, stop!"

"Huh?" Roberto's head snapped up and his eyes met his son. His eyes were glassy and pink, tears flooding down his cheeks. His hands gripped the black rubber grip handle and the deadly end of the weapon was pointed dead at his father's chest, as it rose and fell with every breath that he took. *"Mi ho, just wat in dee fuck do ju plan on doin' wit dat, huh? You plan on shootin' me ova dese, bitch?"* he kicked his mother in the stomach and she doubled over on the floor, holding her stomach. *"Me ya padre, lil' nigga; ju clothes, shoes, video games, motorbike, I bought all dat sheet,"* he spoke to him as he staggered in his direction trying to keep upon his feet.

"Poppa, stop please!" he hollered and cried, snot bubbling out of his left nostril. His four foot eleven frame shook uncontrollably and he felt his bladder growing hot. He was so scared that he about to piss on himself but he had to stand his ground, not just for his mother but for himself. When his father wasn't going upside his head then he was sticking his foot up his mother's ass. Sometimes she would take the beatings for him, getting pummeled like she'd stolen from him.

"Ju don't tell me what to do, Tristan, I'm ya poppa. You do as me say, lil' muddafucka!" he barked, spittle flying out of his mouth. He walked towards him with a threatening expression, slobber hanging from his bottom lip. "And I say put dat pistola down fa I beat cha ass!"

"No!" he hollered back, tilting his head and glaring at his old man. He gripped the revolver tighter, poised to pull the trigger. The light in the ceiling deflected off of its barrel causing it to gleam.

"What ju gone do, huh? Fuck you gone do wit dat puss ass gun?"

"I'ma shoot chu!" he shot back, peering at him with eyes that dared him.

"Well, ju gone have to make me a believer, cabrone. Arghhhh!" He hollered out as he charged forth, about to swing the telephone cord at his face.

Tristan shut his eyelids and gritted, his chest pumped feverishly. He called upon God to give him the strength and courage to pull the trigger and he did...Blam! The blowback from the pistol sent his little ass flying backwards and slamming into the wall. He bumped the back of his head and fell to the floor, eyelids narrowed into slits. The little nigga was moaning from the aching at the back of his skull. His head and back had partially gone through the wall behind him.

Roberto wore a face of complete shock. His eyes were wide and his mouth was open like a dead fish. He looked down at his wife beater and saw a gaping hole there. The black space that was there was quickly expanding redness, soaking up the upper half of his undershirt.

"Oh, shit," he touched his wife beater and his fingers came away with blood. Rubbing his index finger and thumb together, he looked up at his son and then to his

mother. *"Maria, this lil' muddafucka really shot me."* With that, his eyes rolled up to the back of his head and he dropped down to his knees before falling hard as fuck on the side of his face. His back rose and fell as he took his last couple of breaths before he finally went still.

"Papi," Tristan hollered out, fresh tears coating his face. He reached out to his father from where he was sitting up at on the floor. He wished that he could take back what he had done but it was already too late.

"Nooo! Noooooooooo," Maria shrilled at the top of her lungs, clutching the sides of her face. Her tears fell fast and in abundance, veins appearing on her forehead. She was standing on her knees over her dead husband screaming to high heaven seeing him lying lifeless with blood pooling beneath him. *"Oh, God, please don't let this be happening, please, Lord!"*

Tristan shuddered hard seeing what great trauma he had caused his mother. He scrambled upon his feet and ran over to his mother. Getting down on his knees, he embraced her and they sobbed in one another's arms. They shared tears, heartache, turmoil and a cachet of emotions.

Tristan was sentenced to ten years at California's Youth Authority. He didn't receive a visit from his mother because she went bat shit crazy not long after the night he murdered his father. She was put into an asylum. The detention center didn't do goddamn thang to rehabilitate the little nigga. It actually groomed him into an exceptional criminal for when he did touch the streets again. While he was locked up he was spazzing the fuck out up in there. He was robbing niggaz, extorting them, giving them buck fifties across the face and shit, smoking weed, drinking, starting riots. It wasn't until he got the news of his mother's death that he nutted up one last time and beat the shit out of a *correctional officer. That got him put in segregation for a couple of years but he was able to read books. He read every book that was in the library there except the Bible. He had never cracked open the Holy Book, but one night when he was bored out of his mind, he decided to give it a chance. Before he knew it he had read the entire book within a couple of days. Those black words on those white pages were powerful and opened up his eyes to a lot of things. He humbled himself and decided to live his life differently once he did touch the streets. That promise to himself lasted up until he met Eureka and started dating her. He knew the type of shit that she and her brother were into and they weren't willing to let him be in their lives without a little dirt on him.*

Eureka and Anton brought Tristan along with them on a mission that they were contracted to execute. They were to murder a crooked cop that had raped a woman during a traffic stop. Using one gun, they each took shots at the cop until he eventually retired from his existence. Eureka then took the banger and stashed it in a place that only she knew about. This was a murder that they all participated in and if anyone decided to rat then they were all looking at the gas chamber. This was the ritual that Fear had used with them so he could guarantee that he could trust them. From that night forth, Tristan had been working alongside Anton running up them checks as a hit-man for hire.

Present

Tristan's thoughts brought him back to the present day and he focused his eyes on the rearview mirror. Through its reflection he saw Anton opening up the Ziploc bag that his cell phone was sealed inside. Once he recovered his cellular, he flipped it open and dialed up Frost. The phone rang three times before someone picked up.

"Yo, this Shadow," Anton spoke to his employer as soon as he came on the line. "Yeah, I got someone here that wants to say hi." he elbowed Raymar in the stomach and he doubled over wincing, holding himself. "Say watts up to 'em, bitch boy." he twisted his face up when he handed down that command, holding the cell phone to his mouth.

"Watts up?" Raymar croaked painfully.

"You hear that?" Anton held the cellular back to his ear. "Yeah, that's him. Have the other half of my money ready to be sent over. Smooth." he disconnected the call and sat the device beside him. Afterwards, he took out a pair of handcuffs that was in the duffle bag, snapping a cold bracelet on his prisoner's wrist as well as his own. This caused Raymar to look at him with furrowed brows. "If I was you, homie, I wouldn't open my mouth right now." he gave him a firm warning which shut him the fuck up real quick.

"Yo, Ant, you good back there?" Tristan glanced from the windshield to the rearview mirror.

"Yeah, it's all good, my nigga, just slide me to drop this fool off. I'm tryna get paid." he admitted.

"Alright, well, let's dump these burners and get this truck offa the road, this bitch hot ass a firecracker."

"Cool." he pushed his burner into his capture's side and whispered a firm warning into his ear. "You hear me, huh?"

"Yeah, I hear you." Raymar responded depressingly. He knew that his ass was in for it, especially after what the fuck he had done to that CO back in prison. After he'd done her wrong he found out later that her father was a made-man and was connected to some pretty important people.

His antennas were up instantly then because he was expecting the heat to come down on him hard, just as soon as he made his transition to the next prison.

CHaptER 9
Meanwhile

Fear hopped out of the back of the police van as soon as Anton and his squad pulled away from the scene. He held his hand above his brows and peered ahead through narrowed eyelids. There were several police cruisers heading his way with their sirens blaring. With everyone gone he knew that he was on his own and if he wanted a fighting chance he'd need some heat. With that in mind, he dipped off to the driver side door and busted the glass with his elbow. He stuck his hand through the busted out window and unlocked the door. He reached inside and grabbed the shotgun. Turning around, he cocked the shotgun and looked ahead. The heat was coming at him and fast.

Fear pulled his shirt from off of his back and pulled it over his head so that only his eyes would be shown through the neck opening. Having done this, he gripped the shotgun and darted off into traffic. The killer spotted a white and royal blue, souped-up '96 Honda Civic with a spoiler kit speeding up the block. The mothafucka looked like something out of The Fast and Furious movies. He pointed his powerful weapon at the area of the windshield that the driver would be sitting on. The vehicle screeched to a halt and he ordered the Asian nigga sitting behind the wheel out of that mothafucka out. Dude hopped out of his whip and hauled ass across the boulevard, nearly getting hit by oncoming cars. Fear didn't waste any time hopping behind the wheel and slamming the door shut. Soon after, he was speeding off.

****

Eureka rode on Anton's motorcycle against the current. The wind ruffled her clothes and caused the collar of her shirt to flap against the side of her face rapidly. Glancing at her side view mirror, she saw that her brother and husband was a couple of cars behind. Seeing this, she settled down and sighed with relief. She hated herself having gotten her hands dirty yet again, but gave herself a pardon considering the hard truth. Her baby brother was in trouble and she had to help him out of his jam. In saving him she broke an oath that she'd made to herself many years ago. All of this time she thought for sure that she would never have to break it, especially since they had brought Tristan into their little outfit. But here she was four years after the fact and she had just added a couple of more bodies under her belt, staining her hands that much darker with blood.

Eureka shut her eyelids briefly and shook her head. When she peeled them back open she said, "Lord, forgive me for breaking my oath, and please see that it was a necessary evil."

Flashback

"Arrrrrrrr!" Eureka threw her head back hollering in pain. Instantly Tristan shoved a bandana into her mouth and told her to bite down on it which she did. She was sweating like hell and Anton was digging inside of her thigh trying to pull out the bullet that she'd caught. Eureka was laid out on the kitchen table with a balled up T-shirt propping up her head. Her cargo pants were pulled down around her ankles making her silk, off white panties visible.

"You got that shit yet, man?" Tristan frowned, asking Anton with concern. He looked from his woman to her brother panicking. His bloody hand was gripping his wife's. The wedding bands on their finger were stained crimson.

"Grrrrrrrr!" Eureka threw her head back further and arched her back. She squeezed her man's hand even tighter.

"I almost got it, my nigga," Anton assured his brother in law. Removing the bullet out of his sister's thigh had his sole attention. He was dressed in all black and wearing latex gloves. A tin bowl was at his knees as well as a bowl of hot water with steam rising from it. "Reka, you gon' have to hold still if I'ma get this mothafucka outta you, okay?" She looked at him and nodded yes fast, laying her head back on the rolled up T-shirt.

"Hold on." Tristan told his brother in law. He ran off to get some liquor and came back with a bottle of Captain Morgan, his reddened hands twisting off the cap. Once he threw the cap aside, he passed it to Eureka. "Here drink as much of this as you can." she snatched the bottle from him and took it to the head, guzzling it thirstily. Her face balled up tasting the clear alcohol, it burned her throat but she knew without a shadow of a doubt that it would aid her in numbing her excruciation. She swallowed the liquor down and passed the bottle back to her man. He sat the bottle aside and gripped his woman's hand. Once he kissed it and patted it affectionately, he looked into her eyes. He gave her a nod and she returned it. This was confirmation that he had her back, always and forever.

Tristan looked to Anton and gave him a nod to finish pulling out the bullet. He nodded back and went about the task of removing the bullet from his wound. Eureka squirmed and bit down harder on the bandana, squeezing her man's hand tighter. She banged the heel of her boot against the kitchen table, feeling the metal instruments dig deep into her wound.

"*Grrrrrr!*" *Eureka balled her face tighter, drawing wrinkles.*

"*He's almost there, baby, just hold on.*" *Tristan looked from his lady's pained face to Anton.*

"*Got it,*" *Anton smiled triumphantly having gotten the slug out of his sibling's thigh. He held it up and the light reflected off of it, causing it to twinkle. The metal, crimson stained bullet hit the tin bowl with a ting when he dropped it into it. Afterwards, he went about the proceedings of dressing up the wound. While he was performing this task, Tristan dabbed the beads of sweat from off his sister's forehead and kissed the side of her head. It was evident from the look on her face that she was drained from the procedure.*

"*All done,*" *Anton stood to his feet and pulled off his blood stained latex gloves, tossing them into the trash can. Next, he picked up the bowl and went to go rinse it out, leaving the love birds alone.*

"*Where's...where's Kingston?*" *Eureka asked, biting down on her bottom lip to combat the pain as she sat up on the table.*

"*He's in his room asleep, babe. Here, let me help you put on your pants.*" *he said, having seen her struggling to pull them up over her tender wound. Grabbing her hands, he helped her down from the table and kneeled down, pulling up her pants carefully. When the waistband brushed against her wound she grimaced and sucked her teeth. Having gotten her pants around her waist, he zipped and buttoned them up.* "*There you go.*"

"*Thanks, hubby.*" *she kissed his lips and pulled a black bandana from her back pocket. She pulled her hair back into a ponytail and tied it around it. Once she limped over to the kitchen sink, she turned on the faucet and* allowed the cold water to flow freely. She got her hands good and soapy before rinsing them off under the water. Turning the faucet off, she looked up and saw her worrying husband through the reflection of the window. She mustered a weak smile for him to let him know that she really was okay. He returned it.

That night was the closest Eureka had been to death. She and Anton had been contracted to shut down a trap house. They had successful raided the spot and made niggaz vacate, or so they thought. The brother and sister pair were busy stuffing kilos of cocaine into pillowcases when a lone soul came bursting out of the living room closet, blazing. Anton managed to dive for cover, but unfortunately, his sister caught a hot one in her thigh. The gunner, figuring that he had successful laid out Anton, moved in for the kill on Eureka; he found himself standing over her about to deliver the kill-shot when his brains went splattering against the wall. His body went sailing back catching more bullets to its torso. Anton popped two more shots in his bitch ass before helping his sister to her feet and making a hasty getaway from the murder scene.

"Hey, hey, hey," Eureka closed the distance between her and her husband, seeing the worry written all over his face. He appeared to be shaken up.

"Yeah?" he looked up into her eyes as she cupped his face with her delicate hands.

"Are you alright?" she wondered.

"No. Baby, I was scared to death, I thought I almost lost you." he replied with glassy eyes. There was so much blood on their clothes when she and Anton had gotten home that he thought the worse. He relaxed a little once he saw that it was only a wound to her leg and the bullet had *missed a major artery. Otherwise, her little ass would be laid up underneath a sheet with a tag on her toe.*

"I know, boo, but I'm alive and I'm home."

"Thank God." he kissed her and embraced her, squeezing her in his strong arms. The way he was hugging her it seemed as if they were lovers who hadn't seen one another in quite some time.

"Do me a favor, sweetie." she held his hands and stared up into his pretty brown eyes.

""Sup, slim?"

"Draw me a bath; I'm finna go check on Kingston."

"Okay." he kissed her once more before heading off to do what she'd asked of him.

Eureka journeyed up the spiral stairs and entered her son's bedroom. Leaning over into his crib, she smiled and her eyes lit up. She found him sleeping peacefully. After what she had experienced that night, she couldn't wait to have him in her arms. So she scooped him up and carried him across the room, where she sat down in a rocking chair. The chair moved back and forth as she sung him a lullaby.

"...And if that mockingbird don't sing, momma's gonna buy you a diamond ring..." She suddenly stopped, having felt someone at the door. It was Anton. He came strolling in casually, eyes focused on his sister and nephew, a grin on his lips.

"My nephew is beautiful." he peeked over at him.

"He's the most beautiful thing in the world...and he's all mine." She looked upon her baby boy in amazement. She absolutely adored him.

"Damn, to think we could have lost you tonight," he shook his head. If that would have happened he would have

kept homeboy alive for as long as he could, torturing his mothafucking ass. "Sis, I..."

"I'm out." she blurted before he could finish.

"Out?" his forehead scrunched not knowing exactly what she meant.

"Yes, I'm turning my back on this shit; I gotta stay alive for the sake of my family."

He took a deep breath, hating to hear that she wasn't going to be by his side anymore. They were a team and now she was talking about breaking them up. "I could have gotten killed tonight, baby boy. Think about it, Ant, what if that niggaz would have sent one through my heart or my head? I'd be dead, and Tristan would have been left to raise Kingston alone. I don't want my son growing up without his mother." Tears ran down her face. His heart pained to see her cry, so he whipped out his bandana and dabbed her tears away.

"You're right. Nephew is going to need his mother." Anton agreed. "I can hold it down on the solo tip."

"You won't have to," Tristan spoke from the door and they looked his way. "I'll ride witchu. I can save up the loot for us to get our own spot and earn my keep here."

"Bruh, I already told you that I..."

Tristan threw his hand up and stopped him cold. "I'ma grown ass man and I'm not about to let another man take care of my family. I'm not having it. I can either run up a check with you, or get back out in these streets and get it how I live. Shit, I done got it outta the mud before, ain't a thang to me," he folded his muscular arms across his chest and leaned his tall frame against the doorway.

"Alright, big bruh, I'ma give you a play."

"'Preciate that, dawg." he gave him a nod.

The men of the family focused back on Eureka, watching silently as she continued to sing to a sleeping Baby Kingston.

Present

Fear punched out, flooring the gas pedal. The red hand of the speedometer spun around to the other side, and the engine sounded like a grizzly. He dipped in and out of lanes, nearly clipping the side of cars in traffic. Some people honked their horns while others hollered out insults. He didn't pay those niggaz any mind though. Fuck nah, he was a man possessed on a mission.

The killer moved his head from left to right trying to see if he could spot the vehicle that Anton had left the crash site in. All the while doing this, he picked his shotgun up from the front passenger seat and sat it on his lap. An evil smile emerged on his lips when he made the car that his nemesis was in up ahead. He thought that he may see Eureka on the motorcycle but she was nowhere in sight. It didn't matter though, because she wasn't who he wanted. Nah, that nigga Raymar Anton was riding with was who he had his sights set on.

Fear got a firmer hold on the handle of his weapon and prepared to get off. A Mac truck that was driving over into the next lane threatened to close him off from reaching his enemy. Seeing this, he cut off the car in front of him and zipped beside the truck before it could shut him out. He made it just past the truck and avoided an accident. He didn't even bother to glance over his shoulder. This nigga was that bad ass. He had been taking risks. That's why he was called Fearless.

Fear ripped up the street making the lines in the road look like blurs. His head snapped from the windshield to the car that Anton, Tristan and Raymar were riding in. Tristan's

154

looked alive when he saw him and grabbed his AK-47. Both of the men looked between their windshields and one another, wearing hard faces. Suddenly, Anton and Raymar looked over into the ride that Fear was in and were surprised to see his black ass there. Once again the hit-man punched out and sped up ahead. He whipped his car around so that he was facing his enemies and driving backwards. He stuck his shotgun out of the driver side window and got busy with the massive tool.

Bloom! Bloom! Bloom!

Sparks exploded out of the black barrel of the large black weapon. The impact from the blasts cracked the windshield of his rival's car and put what looked like a million holes in its hood. Fear looked back and forth between the windshield and the rearview mirror having gotten off three shots. Tristan brought his head back up having narrowly avoided the blasts meant to take off his fucking head. He smashed out the ruined windshield of his ride with the butt of his assault rifle, and then turned it around. Once he pointed that bastard at Fear's whip he twisted up his face and said, "Is this what chu won't, mothafucka? Well, here it go!"

Ratatatatatatatatat!

The AK-47 bucked wildly in his grip as it regurgitated high caliber rounds and spat empty shell casings out from the slot in its side. The barrel of the weapon shot flames and tatted up the car that Fear was inside. The bullets tore the fucking hood off of the vehicle and shattered the windshield completely. When Fear came back up, he took a shot at Tristan to distract him and then aimed at the tire on the front driver side of his whip. He pulled the trigger and blew the tire to shreds. The vehicle swerved to the left and Tristan grabbed the steering wheel with both hands. He tried to gain control of the vehicle but it was too late. The mothafucka ended up flipping over twice and sliding down the street on its rooftop. Fear tossed his shotgun onto the front passenger seat and slammed down on the brake pedal. The stolen car came to a sudden halt and he threw it in drive, mashing the pedal. The vehicle growled like the beast that it was and zoomed towards Tristan's car.

Fear brought his car to a screeching halt. He grabbed his shotty and threw open the driver side door. As soon as his booted feet touched the pavement he was en route towards the ride that he flipped. Approaching, he saw Tristan hanging upside down struggling to unbuckle his safety belt. Seeing Fear coming in his direction, his head darted around for his AK-47. When he saw it amongst the littered glass of his windshield, he reached out to grab it but only his fingertips managed to graze it. Right then, a shadow eclipsed him and he looked up. Fear kicked the assault rifle far away from his reach. It went spinning around in circles and skidding across the ground. For a time the men stood there locked in one another's eyes, one contemplating if he should kill and the other wondering if he was about to die.

The sudden sound of a back door creaking open and loose glass raining out into the street, stole the killer's attention and set him in the route in which the noise came. When he rounded the car he found a dazed Anton struggling to pull a barely conscious Raymar upon his feet. The young gunner turned around and was surprised to see his nemesis there. The seasoned killer had the stock of his shotgun braced against his shoulder and aimed at his old student.

"Let 'em go, Ant!" Fear commanded.

"Fuck you!"

156

"I'm not playing witcho lil' ass," he barked. "Let 'em outta those cuffs 'fore I turn that ass into road kill!"

"Fear, no!" Eureka shouted from behind them. Fear's eyes darted to their corners, but went right back to Anton.

Eureka stood beside her motorcycle with her AK-47 aimed dead at his mothafucka dome piece. Her eyes were glassy because she never thought that she would be placed in this position, a position where she would be forced to choose between her brother and her lover. "Please, Fear, let 'em go....For me."

"I'd do anything for you, Reka, but I'm not letting yo' brotha go anywhere with my meal ticket." he swore to her. He had a strong hold on his shotgun and his finger was itching to squeeze the trigger. If Anton didn't do like he had ordered him to then he was going to lift that ass straight up out of those boots he was wearing. "If he wants to live to see another sunset then he's gonna have to let my man there go!"

"I'm not letting go of shit, nigga. Suck dick and die," Anton hurled the insult and wagged the bulge in his pants at him. The youngster didn't have any problems killing or dying. This was because he was Fearless, just like the nigga that had trained him.

"That's how you want it, homeboy?" Fear roared. "You remember that I'm the one that taught cho lil' punk ass, no hesitation, you remember? No mothafucking hesitation." he racked the shotgun, and although Anton didn't flinch, that nigga Raymar swallowed the lump of nervousness inside of his throat. He looked between the two killers wondering what was going on and if he was going to fuck around and catch some hot shit.

"Anton…" Eureka called out to her sibling.

"Anton nothing, fuck this nigga," he smacked his hand up against his chest. "You gon' kill a nigga then go ahead, but this snitch ass nigga right here," he held up his handcuffed wrist which brought up Raymar's as well. "He ain't going nowhere unless it's over my dead body." he kept his eyes on his rival and spat on the ground.

"Right," Fear slightly lifted his shotgun so that it would be aimed straight at his chest.

"Fearrrrrrr!" Eureka called out. She was crying now. The tears were literally pouring down her cheeks.

"What?" he hollered out, but kept his eyes and his weapon on Anton.

"Don't do this, don't put me in this position where I have to kill you, please," she sniffled and wiped her snotty nose quickly with the back of her fist. "He's my brother and I love him. I love you too, but when it comes to making a decision...You already know who I'll choose. So, please, please, don't kill my brother." her eyes obscured as tears accumulated in them and went flying down her cheeks.

"Like I said, if this lil' nigga doesn't unass that stooge he's sitting on, then I'm gonna flip 'em." Fear promised. "I'm gonna give you 'til the count of three. One..."

"Anton, let 'em go, okay? Just please let 'em go so we can go home." she looked up at her brother with pleading eyes that were steadily running with tears. She licked them off of her lips and tasted the saltiness of them. For a time Anton didn't say anything. He just stood there staring at his sister and knew that he didn't want his death to upset her like the ones of their parents. With that thought going through his mind, he took a deep breath and pulled the handcuff key out of his pocket. He unlocked the handcuffs and shoved Raymar forward. He came running up to Fear who instructed him to get into the car that he had stolen and drive it backwards to come get him. While he went off to do this, the killer kept his eyes and his shotty trained on Anton. The car he'd stolen came to a halt beside him and the driver side door flew open. Raymar slid over into the front passenger seat and waited for him to get in. Fear slowly got into the car behind the wheel and slammed the door shut. He made eye contact with Eureka and she mouthed 'Thank you'. He gave her a nod and punched it the fuck up from out of there. As soon as he swerved the car around, he threw it in drive and zipped up the street.

Seeing that Fear was finally gone, Eureka lowered her weapon and took a very much needed deep breath. Next, she wiped her forehead with the back of her hand and jogged up the street toward her brother. As soon as she reached him she hugged him lovingly and kissed the side of his face.

"Are you, okay?" she asked concerned, rubbing the side of his face. He nodded yes and took her hand down from his cheek. She could tell that he was pissed from the look on his face but she didn't care. The way she saw it, if she didn't get him to stand down then Fear would have surely blown him away. If there was one thing that the killer upheld it was keeping his word and staying true to his beliefs.

Anton ducked down to get his duffle bag out of the truck. While he was doing so, Tristan was standing upright having just gotten out of the SUV. He held his AK-47 with one hand while the other massaged the back of his neck, as he bent his neck from left to right.

"You good?" Eureka wondered about his current state as she examined him for injuries.

"Yeah, I'll be fine." he winced and bent his back. He was starting to feel stiff after the crash.

"Y'all can take it home on the motorcycle," Anton told them as he hoisted the strap of his duffle bag over his shoulder. "I won't be coming in any time soon tonight so don't stay up waiting." he glanced over his shoulder and placed a hand over his brows, seeing several police cruisers heading in their direction. "Y'all gon' and go, I'll be alright."

"Where are you going?" Eureka's forehead wrinkled.

Anton didn't say a word. He darted across the street looking both ways as his sister continued to call after him.

"Anton...Anton...Anton!"

That night

Anton scaled the mountain of the cabin where Fear had trained him and Eureka. Once he finally reached the top he was hotter than a mothafucka and dripping sweat everywhere. He wiped his forehead with the back of his hand and pulled out his canteen. He screwed off the cap and guzzled it, as he stared up at the full moon. It was big and bright, glowing against the ebony sky. He licked his lips and journeyed on toward the house. When he came upon the steps he flipped up the welcome mat and obtained the key. He let himself in and dropped his backpack and equipment off inside of the living room. He looked at the clock and saw that it was almost time. Hurriedly, he showered and got dressed in all black. He donned a thermal, cargo pants, combat boots and gloves. Lastly, he secured a black bandana around his head and tied it firmly. After he sheathed his bowie knife on his hip, he jogged down the steps and rounded the cabin. He made it over to the space where Fear had fought a wounded and starving mountain lion four years ago. Pulling up the sleeve of his thermal, he glanced at his watch and saw that it was time. It was 8 o'clock on the dot: the time that he and his old mentor agreed upon for their death match.

Anton stood there for a time waiting for Fear to show face. Hours went by with him pacing, throwing rocks at trees, sitting on a log, shadow boxing and doing pushups. Once he looked at his watch again and saw that two hours had passed, he climbed up to the roof of the cabin. He stood at the edge of it with the moon just above his head, lighting him.

The young gunner balled his fists and looked up at the moon like a howling wolf screaming at the top of his lungs, "Cowarrrrrd!"

Anton's voice echoed throughout the mountains turning the heads of several animals in the woods. A deer lifted its head from the pond of water that it was drinking from and looked up in the direction that the voice resonated from. An owl in a shaded tree that could barely be seen looked also. A snake had stopped slithering. A tarantula stopped its movements and a mountain lion looked up from where it was walking in the darkness.

Not too far away

Raymar sat in the front passenger seat of the car with the radio playing. The volume was low, but it didn't matter because he wasn't the least bit interested in the music that was playing. Nah, his attention was focused on the back of Fear. The killer was standing in the front of the vehicle with his hands in the pockets of his jacket. He was staring up at the moon, the same moon that held Anton's attention. He had heard him scream 'Coward' at the top of his lungs and had been tempted to go show him just how much of a

161

fucking coward he really was, but eventually decided against it.

"Fuck 'em, fuck 'em," keeping his scowling face on the moon, Fear spat on the ground and retreated back to his stolen vehicle. The racing car purred like a kitten and slightly vibrated as it idled. Its latest owner opened its driver side door and climbed inside of it, slamming the door shut. He hit the headlights and pulled off.

Raymar's face twisted as he looked back and forth between Fear and the area that he was leaving. He couldn't help but wonder where the hell he was going being as that he was aware of him having to fight Anton until death at 8 o'clock that night.

"What's up?" he asked curiously.

"I'm falling back."

"Falling back?" Raymar's forehead creased.

"Yeah, nigga, 'falling back.'"

With the harshness of Fear's delivery, Raymar knew it was best to leave things be so he sunk down in his seat and focused his attention out of the window, watching the scenery of the mountains pass him by in flashes.

Chapter 10

The next morning

Anton lay over the side of his bed bouncing a blue ball up and down on the hardwood floor. His head had been throbbing something crucial and his body ached having gone so many rounds with Fear the past couple of days. The young killer had been beating himself up since the day he allowed Eureka to talk him out of releasing Raymar into his sworn enemy's custody. He wanted so badly to show that nigga Fear that he wasn't the only one that didn't give a fuck about life or death. He had this in mind and had planned to follow through with it until he seen the pain in his sister's eyes and the tears soaking her face. He didn't know what it was about his sister suffering, but it always got the best of him. It stirred something inside of him that made him want to love and protect her. That was the reason why he folded that day even though he wished that he hadn't.

Anton snatched his ball out of the air this time when it came up from bouncing off of the floor. His head shot up and he snapped his fingers remembering that he'd shot Fear's car with a tracking device when he stole Raymar back from him. He jumped up off of the bed and darted to his nightstand. Quickly, he rummaged through the drawer until he found a black device that looked like a small cell phone. It was a locator to the tracking device. On the screen there was a red dot moving in an upward direction. A wicked smile went across his face. He stashed the device in his pocket and ran into the bathroom. He opened the medicine cabinet in search of a bottle of Excedrin for his headache. Finding the bottle, he popped the top with his thumb and dumped two out into his palm. He tossed two of them back and turned on the faucet water. He used the water to wash the pills down and splashed some onto his face.

"Anton." she spoke from over his shoulder.

"'Sup?" he squeezed his eyelids shut and felt around blindly until he came across a towel.

"Are you really gonna kill 'em?"

"Yep." he said like murder wasn't a thang and then dried his face off.

"Are you sure you wanna go after this nigga?"

Her saying this caused a rage to explode from deep inside of him.

"Yeah, I'm sure. This mothafucka murdered my daddy, my goddamn father in cold blood," he spazzed the fuck out and threw the towel aside, "Turned me and my sister's world upside down."

"Baby boy, I understand you're upset, but…"

"But nothing, I don't know why I'm even entertaining this conversation with you."

"Because you love me, that's why?" she told him what she believed. "You couldn't let me go and I couldn't see myself leaving you."

"Fuck you! I don't need you, you can go about yo' business right now." he screamed so loud that the veins bulged at his temples. "Leave me be and see If I shed one," he threw up a finger, "One, single, solitary goddamn tear over you!" He hung his head and hunched over the porcelain sink, gripping both sides of it. His shoulders rose and fell as he took deep breaths. He felt hotness around his neck and ears. His mothafucking blood was boiling and bubbling. The young nigga was desert sand hot, but was trying his damndest to keep himself under control.

Hearing the woman's sniffling and crying, Anton's head snapped up and he found himself staring at the loaded shelves of the medicine cabinet.

"So this...this is how you talk to...to…"

He slammed the medicine cabinet mirror shut and said, "My mother?" he came face to face with a weeping Giselle.

Flashback

"Why?" Eureka asked, wiping her wet face with the back of her hand as she held the Glock on her mother.

Giselle wiped away the tears that spilled from her eyes with her fingers and thumb. She looked up at her daughter with pink, glassy eyes. She sniffled, "What's that, baby?"

"Why did you?" Her voice cracked. The pain in her heart clogged the words in her throat stopping them from being said. A fresh set of tears ripped down her face and she wiped them away, just as fast as they appeared. She took a deep breath and gathered her wits. She closed her eyes and peeled them back open, feeling renewed. "Why did you have daddy killed?"

Giselle locked gazes with her daughter and she drew in her thoughts. She knew her thoughts like she was a psychic or something. Giselle hung her head. Her teardrops trickled hastily and splashed upon the table-top. Her daughter lay back in her chair with her eyes wide and her mouth open, she was stunned. She looked away with tears dancing in her eyes. She wiped them away before looking to her mother again.

"Money." Giselle uttered.

"Really, ma? Over money?" She couldn't believe it. "How much, huh? How much was my father's life worth to you?"

Giselle looked back up at her daughter, sniffling and wiping her face with her sleeve.

"A million dollars."

"A million dollars, huh?" She sighed and shook her head. "My daddy was worth more than all of the money in the world."

"I know, baby. I know." Giselle shook as she sobbed and whimpered. "I'm sorry; I'm so sorry, baby."

"What happened to the money?"

She shook her head regretfully. "I didn't see a dime of it."

"What?" Eureka sat up in her chair.

"The policy had lapsed," Giselle confessed, her voice cracking with emotion. She'd done a horrible thing that she couldn't take back. If she could, she'd gladly cash in her life so that her late husband could have his. As bad as she wanted it to go that way she knew that it was impossible. He was gone and he wasn't ever coming back.

"Oh, my God," Eureka cupped her hands to her face, as tears poured down her cheeks.

"My guess is your father couldn't afford to pay for it."

"Oh, noooo!" She shook her head sadly.

"I'm sorry, baby girl, if I could take it all back I would. I swear to Christ I would."

"Right. It's too late now, though." Her eyebrows arched and her nose scrunched. She looked like she'd been driven mad with cheeks slicked wet by tears. She wagged the Glock, signaling for her mother to finish with the shot. She didn't feel any sympathy for her mother. She'd been getting a pass for far too many years with her being an addict, widow and single mother, but not anymore. She had made her bed so she had to lay in it.

Giselle swallowed hard and smacked her arm until a thick vein formed. She then picked up the syringe of poison. She looked up into her daughter's face and met a pair of unforgiving eyes and twisted lips. She was looking for mercy but she sure as hell wasn't going to get it from her. Giselle looked back down at the vein in her arm as she pierced it with the needle. Blood rushed inside of the syringe and tainted the liquid the color of malt liquor. Suddenly, her head bobbed as she broke down crying, tears splashing on her tracked up arm.

"Baby girl, I swear to God."

"I don't wanna hear that shit, do it!" Eureka roared, tears cascading and rolling under her chin. She stood up and pointed the burner at her mother's face. Tightening her jaws, she spoke through clenched teeth, "Do it goddamn it, or I swear on his grave I'll open your fucking forehead up, right this minute!"

Giselle looked to Anton and he turned his head. There wouldn't be any sympathy from him either.

Sniff! Sniff! Sniff!

"Okayyy." Giselle whined, wiping her eyes and dripping nose with the back of her hand. She licked her chapped lips and mustered up the courage to do the deed. Finally, she pushed the liquid into her bloodstream. A moment later, her body went through a tantrum that threw her back in her chair. Her arms and legs thrashed around and her head shook violently. Thick foam oozed out of her mouth while blood ran out of her eyes and ears. Giselle's was jerking so hard and fast that she fell out of the chair and landed on the floor.

Thud!

Eureka lowered her banger at her side as she watched her mother's dying form take its last twitches. All *she could do was stand over her as the tears slowly rolled down her face and dripped onto the floor, hitting the tip of her Timberlands. Once Giselle went still, she turned around to Anton and spread her arms.*

"Ant..."

He rushed over to her and wrapped his arms around her tightly. She cried her heart out, tears dripping and staining the shoulder of his shirt. He rubbed her back and encouraged her to let it all go.

"That's it, sis, release it all. Let that shit go." He consoled her as tears danced in his own eyes.

"Ooooooh, Goddddd." Her sobs became muffled by her face being pressed into his shoulder. "Ahhhhh."

Present

Her eyes were moist and pink. Her nose was also red, like she had a cold or something. "Yes, this is the way I talk to the mother that hired the hit-man that murdered my father. The same mother that let a mad man inside of our home and allowed him to corrupt her daughter, the same mother that allowed her children to go without a roof over their heads, decent clothes on their backs or food in their goddamn stomachs. So, yes, that's how I talk to that mother!" During this speech Giselle hung her head and broke down crying. Her crying grew to sobbing and her shoulders shuddered. "And you got the nerve to cry after all you've taken me and Reka through?" he frowned up. "I wish I would allow myself to feel pity for you. That would be the day. I hate cho black hearted ass, and I'm glad you're dead." When he said this, Giselle's head snapped up and she found herself staring into the remorseless eyes of her only son. Her heart broke all over again. It felt like it did that very day when her daughter murdered her without hesitation. "Fuck you, ma," he spat on the mirror and the nasty goo went sliding down the glass. *Crack!* He slammed his fist into the reflection and it cracked into a cobweb. When he drew his fist back particles of broken glass rained down into the sink. He looked at his knuckles and there was residue on them. He looked to the glass that he'd broken and his mother had vanished.

Anton took one last deep breath and made his exit out of the bathroom.

****

Ding!

The elevator sounded when it reached the underground bunker. The doors divorced and Anton headed for his armory. He stepped before the double doors of the space that his weapons and armor were housed, placing his palm down on a black finger print scanner that was beside it. A red laser panned over it, it beeped, then a green laser panned down it. It beeped again. There was the sound of air compressing and then a large lock coming undone. Right after, the twin black Teflon doors slid apart and a light came on, showcasing a variety of weapons hanging on walls behind bulletproof casings. At the far wall, incased in glass, were several mannequins wearing suits of armor and ski-masks with a big red, crooked S on their foreheads. The young gunner didn't waste any time getting dressed and tooling up. As soon as he was done, he mounted his motorcycle and cranked that bitch up. All of its colorful lights came on and he took off. Murder was on his mind and malice was in his heart.

Anton was on his way to make Fear pay for his sins.

****

Tristan and Eureka stood hunched over the kitchen table. An envelope was at the center of them. Their eyes were focused on it.

"Is that what I think it is?" Tristan inquired. Eureka had just came back from the mailbox. Besides a host of bills there was a letter that they both were looking forward to coming in the mail. They feared what was inside because it could change their lives...Forever.

"Yes. I'll open it, but only if you wish me to. Otherwise, I'll turn on the burner of the stove and let the information it contains go up in smoke. You, me and Kingston can go back to being a family and pretend that this never even happened. It's all up to you."

"Just like that? We can go back to how it used to be?"

"Yes." She nodded.

Tristan looked down at his wedding ring and then up at the ceiling. He shut his eyelids and took a deep breath, combing his hand through his crown of dark curls. In that instance glimpses of he and his family went through his mind. Their good and bad times that they'd shared. All he had to do was give his wife the word and the threat of having all of that turned into a nightmare would vanish into thin air.

"Jesus," he blew hard and put his hands on his hips, pacing the floor. He stared at the floor watching his reflection on the kitchen's surface. "This is one hell of a decision I have to make. What about Fear, you think you can get over him?"

"I'll see a therapist." She told him. "I'm sure they'll be able to help me."

He was quiet and still thinking as he continued his pacing of the floor. He had to make a decision and he had to make one now. Suddenly, he stopped his pacing and turned around to her. They locked eyes. It was from this that she knew that he needed to know the truth.

"You sure?" she questioned him.

His shut his eyelids and took a deep breath. He then nodded.

"Okay." She grabbed a steak knife and slit open the envelope. Sitting the knife aside, she pulled out the letter that was stored inside of it. Next, she unfolded the letter and began reading over it. Tristan watched as her eyes became cloudy with tears. She smacked a hand over her mouth and her eyes shifted up from the letter. Her husband's questioning eyes begged for an answer and she gave him one. Instantly, he embraced her and soothed her, rubbing his hand up and down her back. Her body shook as she was racked with emotions. She sobbed into the chest of his shirt long and hard. When she pulled back wiping her eyes, she saw that she'd stained the center of his shirt darker. He told her to hold on and left the room. Once he came back he had a couple of Kleenex tissues which he handed to her. She dried her wet face and blew her nose. From the look on her face it looked like she had a bad cold, with her puffy eyes and red nose.

"Should I..." Eureka went to ask but was cut short by him shaking his head disapprovingly.

"You leave that to me. It's a man thing." Tristan told her. "I think it's best that I engage him being that I'm his father." He kissed her on the forehead and journeyed off to his son's bedroom.

I gotta tell Ant, he should know about this, Eureka thought. She pressed the button on the intercom and called all of the rooms inside of the house, but she didn't receive a response. Afterwards, she ducked off into his bedroom. She knocked before entering and found a note on his bed. She picked it up and read over it.

"Shit, he's going after Fear," She pulled her cell phone out of her back pocket and checked the app on it. She had a direct link to Anton's cellular through a GPS application. This would make the task of finding him very easy. Without a minute to waste, Eureka dashed out of the bedroom to hit the streets. She had to get to her brother before he did something he may regret.

****

Fear was ripping up the road going eighty five miles an hour and leaving debris in his wake. His face held a stern expression as he gripped the steering wheel, foot mashing the gas pedal further and further. His mind was consumed with all of the shit that he had gone through with Anton and Eureka. He couldn't help but think how he had deceived them in keeping away from them that he was the one that had murked their father. The more he thought about all that had happened between them, the more his heart ached. In losing them he had lost the family that he'd yearned for since the passing of his own. If he could do something that could change everything that had happened up to the point where he had pulled that trigger and killed their father, then he would do it. No questions asked. Things were just the way that they were and he was going to have to learn how to cope with them. Otherwise, his demons were going to eat him alive.

Boof!

Fear snapped out of his daydream and looked alive. He looked to the front passenger seat and found a frowning Raymar there. His facial expression was a questioning one.

"What was that?" he inquired.

"I think one of the back tires is blown. Fuck," he slammed his fist down on the steering wheel. Next, he pulled over to the side of the street and threw open the door, jumping out. He made his way to the back of the vehicle and saw that the back tire on the passenger side was flat. He changed the tire and when he went to slam the trunk he noticed a flashing red dot just below it. A line creased his forehead and he took it off of the car, looking at it closely trying to figure out what it was. That's when it dawned on him that what he was holding was a tracking device. Soon after, he realized that Anton had put it there. Hearing someone speeding at his rear, he shot to his feet and whipped around. He saw Anton coming straight at him on a motorcycle with the sun rising over the horizon.

"Shit, it's him, we've gotta get outta here!" Raymar hollered out of the window. For a time Fear stood there not saying anything, just watching his enemy speeding in his direction. "Did you hear me, man? We've gotta go!"

"So leave!" Fear told him without turning around.

"What?" Raymar frowned up.

Fear whipped around and said, "I said, leave, as in get the fuck from up outta here. The GPS is set for the airport and there's a gun in the glove box. I have faith that you'll get there safely."

Raymar looked away and took a deep breath. He then looked back to the hit-man, saying, "Are you sure?"

"Yeah, I'm sure." he gave him a nod.

Raymar threw up a fist and he returned the gesture. With the pleasantries exchanged, the Brazilian native climbed over into the driver's seat and resurrected the Honda. He revved up the vehicle and took off.

Shhhhhhhh!

Anton swung his motorcycle sideways and it skidded to a halt. He kicked up his kickstand and pulled off his helmet, sitting it on the handlebar. He dismounted his bike and stood ten feet away from Fear. He mad dogged him and clenched his fists.

"I've been waiting for this for a looooooong time." he cracked the knuckles on both of his hands.

"You won't be satisfied 'til you kill me, huh?" Fear asked a serious question.

"You mothafucking right," Anton glared at him.

"Well, you'll get no fight from me, lil' brotha," he assured him. "So you gone have to do what chu gotta do." He removed his jacket and pulled off his shirts, leaving himself bare chest.

"Deep down inside you've been a pussy all of this time? I find that hard to believe, big brotha." he stripped down to his bare chest. Now both men were naked from the neck down. They observed one another's muscular forms and noticed that they resembled each others with all of their old wounds.

"Never a pussy, you know betta than that."

"Indeed I do, but this thing right here isn't going to be one sided." Anton's finger jabbed at the ground. "You're gonna fight me like a mothafucking man, right here and right now!"

"If you think killing me is going to make you feel better, then go ahead!" Fear urged his hot headed protégé, sticking out his chin and crossing his wrists at his back.

"No! You fight me like a fucking man!" Anton slammed his fist against his chest hard, gritting. "Shoot me the fair one, may the realest killa win!"

"No. I love you too much to kill you, baby boy." His eyes became glassy, but his face was chiseled out of stone. "I regret the day I ever…"

"Shut uuup!"

Bwock!

A spin kick to the jaw sent his mentor's head whipping around, speckles of blood flying every which way.

"Ooof!" he crashed to the ground on his side, mouth bloody, teeth red, eyes blinking as if he was having trouble focusing his vision.

"No. no. no, I don't wanna hear that bullshit! Fuck your love!" he screamed on him, spittle flying from his lips. "Get cho bitch ass up and fight me like a goddamn man, you fucking coward! Show me the killa that the streets feared and my sister loved!"

"No." Fear shook his head and spat blood on the surface, a length of red saliva hanging from his bottom lip. He winced as he got to his booted feet, wrists still crossed at his back. "I love you, and I'm willing to die for you, right here and right now if it means you finding peace."

"Fight meeeee!" Anton shrilled like a madman, red webs in his eyes and veins pulsating on his neck and temples.

"Nooooooo!" The assassin yelled at the top of his lungs matching his intensity. His eyes stretched wide open, spit clinging to his lips.

"Grrrrr!"

Crack! Crackk! Bwhrack! Thrwack! Shrack! Bwap!

Anton's blows came swift and hard, impacting his old teacher's face and body. Gashes opened on the seasoned killer's cheeks bones, a knot swelled on his forehead and his nose broke, leaving a sore red line. He dropped to the ground several times but kept getting back up to take the punishment he felt that he deserved. The younger killer drew his fist back and got ready. He watched Fear attentively as he slowly got to his feet, trying to regain his equilibrium. As soon as the executioner had both feet planted firmly on the ground, he did one of those famous Jean Claude Van Damme kicks, whipping his head around in a blur.

Wappp!

The youngster landed back on his feet in a fighting stance just as his opponent hit the surface. His gloved fists were bloody. His face was speckled with blood. His heart was raging inside of his chest. "Haa! Haa! Haa! Haa! Fight...Fight me..." he said out of breath, exhausted but determined.

"N...no," Fear breathed with his head angled against the ground. His heavy breathing blew debris from under him as he struggled to get to his feet on wobbly legs, holding his wrists in place. His right eye was swollen shut and the size of his nose had doubled, blood dripping from his bottom lip. The League of Executioners lead assassin was hurting more than he'd ever hurt before, but not from his wounds. Nah, he'd caused one of the people he loved most in life a great deal of pain. To him that ranked up there with betrayal, and under L.O.E's law he had to be sentenced to death.

"Come on!" Anton bellowed, with eyes filled with turmoil and pain. He loved the nigga he was putting hands on like a brother, but his deceiving had crippled him emotionally. He'd given him a father figure to love, and just like that, he snatched it away. This only proved to him that life was a cold hearted bitch without a conscience. Damn!

Fear spat on the ground and shook his head no, holding his chin up for his successor to take another shot at him.

"I said, no, now finish me!"He closed his eyelids and tears came bursting out of his eyes. His tears weren't ones of physical pain but emotions. He wished that the strapping young hit-man before him could feel all of the love he had in his heart for him. Somehow he thought that by letting him beat him to a bloody pulp would knock some sense into him, but so far the taste of blood had only stir awake the killing machine. With that having failed, he could only hope that with him losing his life that his pupil could live the rest of his in peace.

I love you, lil' homie, and I hope with my death you find some sort of tranquility in life.

"Then you die!" he hissed with a scowling face, baring his teeth.

Bwap! Bwapp! Crack! Bwhrack! Bwop!

Fear fell to the ground with a thud with his good eye nearly closed shut, and the side of his face now swelling like he'd been bitten by a poisonous snake. Anton approached him slow and steady, keeping his keen eyes on him. He watched as he wheezed. His face resembled bloody hamburger meat. It was safe to say that he was on his way out.

Anton cracked his knuckles as he advanced in his mentor's direction. He was so focused on him that he was incoherent to the Chevy Impala driving up behind him. It came to a screeching halt at his rear and the driver side door flew open. The vengeful killer grabbed the man that had been as good as family to him by his throat and pulled him forward. Staring into his eyes and studying the pain in his face, his drew his hand back in an Eagle's claw. With this deadly move that he'd been taught by him, one could tear a man's throat out.

"Antonnn!" Eureka screamed and ran as hard as she could, tears misting in her eyes.

Anton's head snapped over his shoulders and he saw his sister coming up from behind him. "Stay back, Reka!"

he shouted her a warning. He then turned his hateful eyes back on the man that he'd been training to kill for years.

"I...I love you, lil' brotha...and I'm sorry for breaking your...your heart." Fear croaked, ready to embrace death like the brave man that he was.

"Don't do it, Ant! You can't!" his sister screamed at his back, still running in his direction.

"Do it, finish me." Fear closed his eyelids, tears steadily flowing. He wore a smirk on his lips. It was about to be over and his little brother's soul could finally rest.

Anton's eyes welled up with tears and spilled down his cheeks, running over his lips. His hand slightly shook as he was drawing all of his strength into it for the Kill Move. Truthfully, he didn't want to do it, but this mothafucka had stolen his father from him. In his mind this had to be done. It was the right thing to do. He couldn't turn back now and set him free. Nah, fuck that, how could he live the rest of his life knowing that he'd let the nigga live that had murked out his old man? It would haunt him until the end of his days, so he had to put this issue to bed now.

"Grrrrrr!"

"Anton, please, you can't kill him!" Eureka slowed to a jog she was so exhausted. She wanted so badly to stop but she had to keep going if she was going to save Fear.

The young assassin's head whipped around to his sister, but he still kept his Eagle's Claw above his head. "Why, huh? Give me, one good goddamn reason why I shouldn't rip this cold hearted bastard's throat out!"

"Because...he's Kingston's father."

CHaptER 11

Tristan cracked open the door of his son's bedroom just enough for him to peer inside with one eye. His forehead creased with lines watching his little man in action. His face was a mask of concentration as he stood before the full body mirror doing all of the martial arts moves that his uncle Anton had taught him. His little arms and legs were moving so fast that they looked like blurs. His face and arms were glistening lightly from perspiration. He was making hissing noises with each and every movement. The way he was going at it, it appeared as if he was fighting someone for real.

Tristan's brows furrowed seeing his son in action. It appeared as if he was in his own world and the only things that existed in it were him and his opponent. He hung back watching the fruit of his loins with curious eyes, thoroughly impressed by what he was seeing before him. He was a black belt himself and he had been teaching the youngster some things, the moves he was displaying weren't of anything that he had taught him, so that brought him to one conclusion: his uncle Anton had been his teacher.

"King!"

Kingston had just did a Round House kick and landed on his bare feet when he heard the sound of his father's voice. Startled, the little nigga gasped and whipped around. His chest leaped up and down as he huffed and puffed feverishly. His forehead was beaded with sweat and his arms were running with witness.

"Yes, dad?" he grabbed the white towel from off his bed and wiped off his face and then his arms.

Tristan peered out of the bedroom to make sure no one was coming before ducking back inside and closing the door behind him. He sat on his son's dresser and folded his arms across his chest.

"Come here for a minute."

Kingston tossed the towel back upon the bed and approached his father timidly.

"Yeah dad?" he looked up at his old man.

"Who taught you that stuff?"

"You did."

He looked him square in the eyes and said, "If you'll lie then you'll steal." Kingston casted his eyes to the floor, but when his father called him his head snapped right up. "Now who taught you?"

"Uncle Ant."

"Uncle Ant?" a line deepened his forehead.

"Yeah." he nodded rapidly. "He said I'm going to be the man of the family, so I have to be prepared when the day comes to defend it."

Tristan took a deep breath and kneeled down to his son, placing a firm hand on his shoulder. "I agree. One day when you have your own family you're gonna have to be able to provide for them and protect them."

"I know."

Tristan smiled, ruffled his son's head and kissing him on it. "You like training with your uncle, huh?"

"Yeah," the little dude's eyes came alive. "He taught me how to fight, hunt, how to tell time by the way shadows are casted, use a knife, shoot…" He stopped there when he saw his father look at him like there was something terribly wrong.

"Shoot?" The skin on Tristan's forehead bunched together.

"I mean, uhhhhh."

"Nah, you said shoot. Your Uncle Anton taught you how to shoot?"

Kingston expelled his hot breath and hung his head, nodding yes. He felt bad having let the secret slip that he made with his uncle. The deal was that he was going to teach him any and everything he knew, but only if he agreed to keep his mouth shut.

"This mothafucka teaching my son to be a goddamn assassin," Tristan gritted and balled his hands into fists, pacing the bedroom floor.

As soon as he laid his eyes on Anton they were definitely locking ass.

****

Julian pulled up before the gates of Anton's estate, looking from left to right at the surveillance cameras homed in on him. Their lenses turned and pushed outward, zooming in on where he was sitting in his vehicle idling. They saw through black and white and detected all of his movements. Seeing this, the European assassin opened his console and pulled out a black device with a blue light that blinked on and off. He pointed it at the windshield before the mansion and pressed the button on it that was located at its lower end. The device beeped and its light turned green.

****

Hearing static throughout the house as a result of Julian's remote control, Tristan stopped his pacing of the bedroom floor. His forehead deepened with grooves as he stared at the flat-screen mounted on the wall. Picking up the remote control, he flipped through the channels and found every one of them filled with static. Finally, he turned off the television and turned the dial of the stereo on. He found that every channel had static too.

"Stay here, son, I'll be right back." he commanded his mini me before making a mad dash out of his bedroom. He stepped inside of Anton's study and looked at the multiple monitors that were linked to the surveillance cameras outside. They all were filled with static. That's when it dawned on him that someone was probably moving in on the mansion. His head snapped towards the tall glass cabinet that housed several weapons. He searched high and low inside of the desk drawers for the keys, but he couldn't find them. A light bulb came on inside of his head and he darted over to the cabinet. Using his elbow, he slammed into the glass until it cracked into a spider's cobweb and eventually gave. Reaching inside, he grabbed a hold of a shotgun and beat the lock off of the pad-locked drawer that was at the bottom of the cabinet. Once he pulled it open he discovered several boxes of ammo. Hastily, he took out a box that matched his weapon and dumped its contents on the floor. He loaded up his shotgun as fast as he could, and then stuffed a handful of shells inside of his pocket. Standing erect, he racked his firearm and found his little boy at the door. He had a worried expression on his face seeing his father with the shotgun in his hands and the scowl painted across his face. The only time he saw him like this was when he was heated and dead ass serious.

"I...I..." Kingston stammered. His tongue moved but he couldn't find the words. He didn't have to, especially with the loud crash stealing his old man's attention.

Boom!

The loud noise brought Tristan and his son's heads around to the study's door. The sound had resonated from outside. At least this is what Tristan had gathered.

"Someone's attacking the mansion; they must have blown down the front gates entrance. Come on," he hoisted his shotgun over his shoulder and grabbed his little man by his hand, running out of the study in a hurry. Entering his bedroom, he opened the closet and stashed him inside. "I'll be right back, son. You stay here until I..."

"No, no, no," he shook his head no rapidly, tears building up in his eyes. "I don't won't chu to go! Let's just leave, we can get outta here together, dad!"

"This is our home, son," he spoke to him sternly, staring him directly in his eyes. "I am the king and you're the prince. We must defend our castle. We must protect our kingdom with our lives. No retreat. No surrender, remember?" he waited for him to repeat the mantra that he had taught him.

"No retreat..." he sniffled and wiped his eyes. "No surrender."

"That's right. Good boy." he ruffled his head and kissed his forehead. He went to leave and he hugged him by the waist breaking down sobbing. He knew that he didn't have much time before whomever had broken in through the gates came charging inside of the house, but he had to provide some comfort for his son before he went charging off into battle. So he threw his arm around him and rubbed his back affectionately. "It's okay, King. It's going to be alright." he held up his chin so that he would be looking up at him. "You hear me?" He nodded yes and wiped his face with the lower end of his shirt. "Good." he held his forehead against his son's and kissed him twice on the forehead before closing the closet door shut.

****

Boom! Boom! Boom! Boom!

The double doors of the mansion rattled and resonated as a powerful force attempted to get inside. Tristan, heart beating, palms sweaty approached the door.

He had the stock of his shotgun braced against his shoulder and the business end of his weapon leveled at the mansion's entrance. His heart pounded inside of his rib cage and bumped up against his chest bone. He didn't know what the fuck was on the other side of those doors, but when it came before his eyes he was going to blow its mothafucking head clean off.

Ba-Boom!

The double doors flew inward and Tristan found a white man clad in body armor and wearing a holster strapped to his thigh that contained a Desert Eagle. Wearing a neoprene mask on the lower half of his facel, and having a form ripe for summer made him look like an action figure. Tristan glanced over the man's shoulder and found a late model Cadillac Seville parked on the lawn. There were tire prints on the pretty green grass and in the background one of the gates was hanging off of its hinges. It came to mind then that the hit-man must have had some sort of gadget to disrupt all electrical devices which was why every electronic device had stopped working inside of the house. This had allowed him access on the estates grounds without being detected.

For a time the men stood where they were mad dogging one another, their chests rising and dropping with every breath that they took. Having grown tired of the stare down, Julian made the first move and that's when Tristan's shotgun roared to life. The impact from the blast lifted the hit-man off of his booted feet and sent him skidding across the porch. Tristan stood there for a time with his shotgun smoking. He waited for the man to get back up, but he never did. Figuring that he'd killed him off, he cautiously moved in on him. He kept his eyes on him and his trigger finger on the ready. Tristan got within three feet of his victim before he kicked him twice to see if he would budge. When he didn't, he sighed with relief feeling that his reign of terror was over. Suddenly, Julian's eyelids snapped open and he peeled his lips apart. Something shiny and silver was clenched between his teeth. He spat it out and three poisonous needles stabbed into his attacker's neck. He winced and staggered back surprised. He threw up the hand that held the shotgun and it blasted off into the sky. Tristan spun around and fell to the ground. He blinked his eyelids uncontrollably and pulled the needles out of his neck. When he looked at them they had blood at the tips of them. Tossing them aside, he scrambled onto his feet and staggered towards the mansion. His blurry vision came in and out of focus as he looked over his shoulder to see if Julian was on his ass, which he was. The hit-man was strolling casually in his direction as if he didn't have a care in the world, whistling Dixie.

"Oh fuck!" His eyes widen seeing that the killer was closing in on him. He nearly fell on his way up the steps, but quickly regained his equilibrium. Crossing the threshold into the mansion, he whipped around with his fists up ready to get active with the perp. "Come on, big boy! Come get these hands!"

Seeing the assassin pull his bow-gun from off his back, Tristan's eyelids shot open and he made off of the porch quickly. He ran as fast as he could, breathing heavily and hoping that he didn't catch one in his back.

"Haa! Haa! Haa! Haa!" he huffed and puffed while hauling ass. He glanced over his shoulder and he saw the hit-man pointing the bow-gun at him. He made to zig-zag and that's when he heard the arrow whizzing through the air. The sound of it zeroing in grew louder and louder as it drew closer. Before he knew it he felt something sharp pierce his back and send him hurtling towards the living room wall. He screamed at the top of his lungs as he flew across the room, slamming into the wall. The impact caused him to wince and caused the portrait of him, Eureka and Kingston to rattle where it hung. The portrait rocked back and forth before falling to the floor and cracking down its middle.

Tristan hollered and screamed trying to push himself off of the wall, but there wasn't any use. He was stuck to the wall like a nail that had been hammered to it. The area of his body that had been punctured by the arrow was quickly being absorbed by blood. He twisted and turned as he gritted trying his damndest to pull himself free. Grabbing the end of the arrow, he tried to pull it out and break it off but he wasn't strong enough. Doing this only succeeded in him causing blood to run down the length of the projectile and slick his fingers wet.

Suddenly, Julian grabbed a handful of Tristan's curly hair and pulled his head back. When he did this, his victim's eyelids turned into slits and he squared his jaws, showcasing the muscles in them.

"Grrrrrrr." he growled like a lion disturbed from its slumber.

"Where is Fear?" Julian asked really slowly. His face was stern and unforgiving.

"Who?" he asked through gritted teeth.

"Fear."

"Oh, Fear. Hold on, let me pull 'em outta my ass." having his head slammed into the wall split his forehead open and a slither of blood ran. His eyes rolled to their whites and his head lulled about. He was moaning and barely conscious.

Julian pulled his head back by his hair again. "Is anyone else here?"

"I'm not...I'm not telling you jack, shit-head!" he gritted.

"Is dat right?"

"Fucking aye." he croaked in pain.

"I'm gonna take it dat neither he, nor Eureka are here. Fine, I guess I'll settle for da boy instead."

"What...what boy?"

"Dis boy." he pulled out a picture of Kingston and brought it before his eyes.

"That's...that's...my...my...son."

"Hmmm, interesting." the killer raised an eyebrow. "Where is he?"

Seeing something flying by at the corner of his eye, Julian's head snapped in its direction. He dropped the picture and drew his knife, throwing it with all of his might. It spiraled in circles heading towards it mark. The blade buried halfway inside of the maid, Alice's, shoulder. She hit the floor hard balling up her face as she felt the pain soaring throughout her shoulder. Taking his time, Julian stashed his bow-gun on his back and made his way toward her. Standing over her, he dropped the picture of Kingston near her face where she could see it.

"Where is dis child?" He asked, mashing the heel of his shoe down on the kilt of the knife in her shoulder, causing her to release a scream so intense that it could burst eardrums.

She rasped out of breath as she attempted to answer him. "I don't...I don't know."

"Wrong answer," He mashed his boot down further against the kilt, pushing the blade deeper into her flesh and making blood flow in a river.

"Arghhhhh," She screamed aloud, showcasing all of the teeth and pinkness inside of her mouth. Tears oozed out of her narrowed eyelids and encircled her face as she dug her fingers into the carpeted floor. He let his boot up off of the kilt and relieved some of her pain. She hung her head and her shoulders hunched up and down as she breathed huskily. She didn't have an idea where Tristan had stashed Kingston because she was trying to find somewhere to hide as soon as she knew some shit was about to pop off.

"Tell me where I can locate da boy, or I shall bring you to ya demise, woman." He snatched the Desert Eagle from out of the holster strapped to his thigh, holding it at his side in his leather gloved hand. He pressed his boot down against the center of her back, pinning her down to the surface. For a second he listened to her moaning and groaning before growing agitated with her response, or lack thereof. "Tell me, tell me now gotdamn it, 'fore I put a bullet in da back of ya bloody skull."

Bringing her head back up she shouted, "Go to hell!"

"You fust, bitch!"

Blam!

The first shot blew half of her head apart, sending brain fragments and red pieces of skull everywhere. Specs of blood speckled the side of the white couch. He leveled his head bussa at her back and gritted, dumping on her and watching her corpse twitch like it was going through convulsions. When he was finished he tucked his smoldering weapon back inside of its holster and pulled the tranquilizer gun from the holster at the small of his back. He pulled a dart from the row of them lining the belt that was strapped around his opposite thigh. After he loaded one into the weapon, he went about the hunt for young Kingston, whistling Dixie as he climbed the stairs. He gently pushed

188

opened door after door, peeking his head inside of each bedroom. Once he found the one that resembled a child's, he made his way inside.

Kingston was still in the back of his parents' closet staring out through the shudder door. The reflection of the outside light shone in on his face. All he could hear was his own heavy breathing as he watched Julian walk back and forth across the bedroom, lifting and turning over shit, looking for his little ass. Abruptly, he stopped at the center of the floor in the path of the closet causing Kingston to hold his breath. His tiny heart was beating so fast that his shirt twitched with its every thump. The hit-man did a slow counter clockwise spin were he stood until he was facing the closet and had locked eyes with the little boy. The youth's eyes bugged and he gasped, stepping back away from the door. He bumped up against the wall, but then his face transformed into a scowl when he remembered when his uncle Anton told him to fear nothing and no one. With that in mind, he clenched his small fists and got into a martial arts fighting stance.

Julian smiled like the cat that had swallowed the canary when he realized his prey was hiding inside of the closet. He licked his lips and started for the door.

"Why there ya are, ya lil' fella," as soon as he turned the knob and opened the door, a battle cry shook his ear drums and Kingston came running at him full speed ahead. The assassin's eyes widen and his mouth hung open. "What da fu…Ooof!" A sharp kick doubled him over causing him to drop the tranquilizer gun and cup his balls. He went cross eyed and groaned, squaring his jaws. The little dude Round House kicked him across the jaw which sent him falling up against the side of the bed wincing. "Ahhhh," Seeing that his predator was out of commission, Kingston took the advantage and hauled ass out of the bedroom, sights set on the staircase. Julian bit down on his bottom lip to combat the pain in his lower region as he scrambled around on his knees, searching for the dart shooting weapon. When he zeroed in on it, a evil smile stretched across his lips. He grabbed it up and took a stance on his knee, extending his weapon and shutting one eye to take aim. He stuck his tongue out of the corner of his mouth, as he waited for the right time to fire. "Run Forest, run," The hit-man spoke in a soft tone, watching the youth run for his life.

"Haa! Haa! Haa! Haa," Kingston ran as fast as he could, huffing and puffing. His heart was beating with a vendetta behind his chest and he hoped he wouldn't be shot. *Please, God, don't let 'em kill me,* he thought as his made tracks like he was in a marathon, eyelids shut, adrenaline pumping like mad through his body.

"Got 'em," Julian spoke to no one in particular as he held his weapon outstretched. His target was almost at the staircase when his finger curled around the trigger.

Pewk!

The dart whistled through the air like an arrow en route to its intended mark.

Haa! Haa! Haa! Haa! Haa!

Kingston bowed his head and squeezed his eyelids tighter, running even faster.

Shhhhhhhhhh!

The dart whistled through the air looking like a blur while in motion.

Haa! Haa! Haa! Haa! Haa!

Kingston couldn't see it, but he could feel its deadly aura around him so he ran that much faster.

Shhhhhhhhhhh!

The dart was twisting around headed in the direction of the youth.

Julian smiled harder looking like a sneaky rodent about the face.

"Dat's ya ass." He just knew he'd gotten him.

Thwack!

His eyes went big and he mouthed '*What the fuck*' when the dart stabbed into the wall. It missed his prey by a mere inch as he made a left, hurrying down the staircase.

How in the hell did I miss? Julian couldn't help thinking.

"Son of a bitch," The UK assassin rose to his feet, pissed off that he'd missed his target. He pulled another dart from the Velcro strap around his thigh and loaded it up, cocking it back. He held his aching balls with one hand as he hurriedly limped along while the other held tight to his tranquilizer gun. Heading down the corridor, he looked over the guard railing to see Kingston halfway down the staircase, "Where do you think ya going, ya brat? Huh?" The assassin made it to the top of the steps just in time to see the youngster reaching the first floor.

Kingston was on his way out of the door when something at the corner of his eye stole his attention.

"Dad?" he frowned up seeing his father impaled to the wall. He made to go help him but his father's yelling froze him in place.

"Get outta here, son, go!" Tristan yelled at him, looking very weak and exhausted from where he was stuck against the wall.

"But dad…" his eyes misted with tears and his bottom lip quivered.

"Please, son, hurry," His pleading eyes urging him to get the hell out of there, "Hurry, run for your life!"

Kingston's eyes lingered on his father for a time longer, his chest swelling and falling with each breath. Abruptly, he took off running out of the house, nearly being hit by the poisonous dart that Julian had launched at him from the top step. The dart stabbed into the door just as Kingston cleared the threshold on his way out. He hurried down the steps making tracks across the lawn. Just then, the European hit-man made it out on the front porch, watching the youngster's back as he ran off, occasionally looking over his shoulder.

Julian lifted his tranquilizer gun and took aim, pulling the trigger. The weapon jerked when it unleashed another tainted dart. It whizzed through the air, seemingly slowly rotating while on course to its target's back.

The impact of the tranquilizer dart caused Kingston to stumble forward and crash to the lawn. He lay there wincing and in the beginning stages of passing out. He pushed up from the ground on wobbly arms. He went to stand to his feet and fell flat on his face. Shutting his eyelids, he took one deep breath and his shoulders fell. The rest of his breaths were calm and steady. A shadow came from behind him and eclipsed his body where it lay limp. Julian pressed his boot against the little nigga'z back, grabbed a hold of the dart and yanked that bitch out. Next, he pulled two pairs of zip-cuffs out and laid one on his back. He used the first pair to cuff his wrists behind his back and the second pair to secure his ankles. Afterwards, he tossed his little ass over his shoulder and carried him off to the rear of his Cadillac. He dumped him inside. Standing over Kingston while he held open the trunk, he observed him for a moment before slamming it shut. He smacked imaginary dust off of his hands and glanced back at the mansion where he saw Tristan continuing his struggle to get off of the wall that he was pinned against.

Julian made his way around his Cadillac and jumped in behind the wheel. He cranked that big bastard up and went on about his business whistling Dixie.

****

Kingston lay in the trunk of Julian's Cadillac bumping around with each dip and pothole the vehicle met. Slowly his eyelids fluttered open and he found himself staring at the red brake lights of the car. He was in darkness save for the outside light that shone through the cracks and crevasses of the vehicle. He tried to move his arm and ankles and found that they were bound. When he went to scream he discovered that his lips were sealed shut by the tape stretched over them. He struggled to get himself lose, and found that the more he did so the hotter it became and the harder it was for him to breathe. Establishing this in his young mind, he figured that it was best for him to lie still until he could think of some other way to get free.

Kingston's face scrunched up and he shut his eyelids, tears bursting through them. He whimpered and his body shuddered uncontrollably. For as brave as he was he was still just a child.

Please, dad, save me, he thought, *pleeeease.*

****

Meanwhile

Tristan gritted and threw his head back. His crimson stained hand clenched the end of the arrow that had him pinned to the wall while he was trying to push off of the wall with his foot pressed against it. More blood traveled down the length of the arrow's shaft and dripped on the floor. His face balled tightly and veins came up his neck and arms, as he strained himself trying to get free to rescue his son.

"I'm coming, son, I'm comiiing," he called out. "Daddy's coming…Grrrrr."

Little by little the arrow began to inch out of the wall.

TO BE CONTINUED…

The Devil Wears Timbs 5

The Game of Death

AVAILABLE NOW BY TRANAY ADAMS

The Devil Wears Timbs 1-5

Bury Me A G 1-3

Tyson's Treasure 1-2

Treasure's Pain

A South Central Love Affair

Me And My Hittas 1- 6

The Last Real Nigga Alive 1-3

Fangeance

Fearless

COMING SOON BY TRANAY ADAMS

The Devil Wears Timbs 6: Just Like Daddy

A Hood Nigga's Blues

Bloody Knuckles

Billy Bad Ass

CPSIA information can be obtained
at www.ICGtesting.com
Printed in the USA
LVHW011743120821
695155LV00014B/1340